Julie Noble studied psychology and literature at Lancaster University. Intrigued by the Brontës she has made extensive studies before writing this book. She is married to Mark and they have three children, one of whom struggles every day with dyslexia and dyspraxia.

J Noble

Julie Noble

Talli's Secret

Matador
9 De Montfort Mews
Leicester LE1 7FW, UK
Tel: (+44) 116 255 9311 / 9312
Email: books@troubador.co.uk
Web: www.troubador.co.uk/matador

ISBN 1 904744 77 X

Cover illustration by the author

Typeset in 10pt Stempel Garamond by Troubador Publishing Ltd, Leicester, UK
Printed by The Cromwell Press, Trowbridge, Wilts, UK

Matador is an imprint of Troubador Publishing

This book is dedicated to everyone who knows
what it is to struggle.

What is the difference between a winner and a loser?
A winner gets up one more time.

Acknowledgements

There are many people who have given inspiration and encouragement to enable me to write and publish *Talli's Secret*.

I am indebted to the following.....

The author G.P. Taylor, who read the manuscript. Although, extremely busy with his own phenomenally successful books, he made time to encourage me not to give up.

The author Simon Jowett, who first made the suggestion that I write a book for children, and kindly read and advised on the very first (rough!) draft.

The Brontë biographer Juliet Barker, whose amazingly detailed work on the Brontës inspired me to include their lives in my book.

Charlotte Brontë and her family, for having a dream, and following it.

To the author who suggested in an article in the magazine of the Dyspraxia Foundation several years ago that Maria Brontë may well be fiction's first dyspraxic.

To the health and educational professionals who work with children who have conditions such as dyslexia and Dyspraxia. I must especially thank those who have worked hard to help my son overcome his own difficulties. Over the years he has developed from a six year-old who dreaded school to the confident young man he is today. Particular thanks must go to Jenny Sammons, occupational therapist, to Mr Geoffrey Loy of Northac International Theatre School, and Mrs Christine Thompson of the Dyslexia Institute.

Thanks to those members of my family and friends who have supported and encouraged the production of *Talli's Secret*, especially after the injury to my right hand, which made typing so difficult.

Finally, thank you to my children, Jessica, Jonathon and Robert, for reading, discussing, commenting on, but, most of all, enjoying Cassie's story.

Last of all, I am eternally grateful to my husband Mark for his belief in me, and his absolute determination to see this book published.

Chapter 1

"Are you listening to me, Cassandra Edwards?" At the sound of her name Cassie snapped out of her absorbing daydream with a jolt, blinking in confusion as she turned to focus on the hard, dark features of the classroom. It was a struggle to perceive what was in front of her instead of thinking of the fleeting impression of sunshine that was still in her mind. As her head cleared she realised, with a sickening lurch of her stomach, that the whole class was staring at her, and Mrs Harrison's face had turned a decidedly pukey puce colour.

"Cassandra!" Repeated the teacher, "I said have you been listening to me?" Cassie blinked again and looked across at Mrs Harrison in genuine surprise; the other children watched with interest and anticipation; they were used to Cassandra's daydreams, they provided a guaranteed source of amusement. Savannah Smythely was the most delighted, she nudged the girl sitting next to her and whispered something, the girl pretended mock horror and exclaimed loudly, "Savvy!" but then they looked at Cassie and started giggling. While Cassie watched, Savannah leaned her chair back to the desk behind her and whispered again. From her seat Cassie could hear the last three words,

"Pass it on."

Murmurs rippled across the class and broke out into a wave of laughter among the boys in the far corner. Mrs Harrison glanced at them swiftly and her eyes narrowed but she said nothing. She wants them to laugh at me,

Cassie thought, and her chin began to ache with the effort of stopping it from quivering. She hoped it wasn't too obvious, if Savannah saw it break time would be torment unless she could find somewhere else to hide, the girls toilets were no good as a hiding place, and Savannah had found all the others. Cassie's eyes began to fill with liquid and she blinked rapidly; Mrs Harrison noticed and sighed.

"For the third time, Miss Edwards, I have to ask: were you listening to me?"

Cassie put her head down and gripped her hands together, hard. Her stomach was twisting backwards and forwards. She was thinking about what her mother had said just that morning at breakfast:

"You must try and do better at school, Cassie. Stop all this nonsense from your silly daydreams and make sure you tell the *truth*." Cassie had nodded sadly, it was impossible to tell her mother that she didn't *know* she was going to daydream, in fact she didn't even know she was in one. until someone snapped her out of it, instead she had promised to try, and Lorna had managed a weak smile.

"Well done, darling." Cassie had hoped for a comforting hug but just then her mum noticed the time on the kitchen clock.

"Look at that! You've got to set off and I've got to give your dad a hand getting dressed." Cassie's face was crestfallen and her mum felt guilty.

"Tell you what; when you come home tonight, we can celebrate when you tell me what a good day you've had." Cassie nodded, she wanted to say something but just then her dad called angrily from upstairs.

"I'm waiting, Lorna. I need you *right now*." The bitterness in his voice grated harshly and Cassie and her mum exchanged awkward glances.

"I'd better go." Cassie said, and grabbed her schoolbag and left. She was halfway down the street when she heard her mother running after her and realised that she had, as usual, forgotten something; today it was her lunch. She watched guiltily as her mother came puffing towards her, Lorna's face was bright red and sweating in the early morning heat, she was flustered and out of breath as she placed the plastic tub into Cassie's hands and looked back quickly, as if she half expected to see her husband crawling down the road after them .

"Sorry, mum." Cassie had said, uselessly.

"Never mind. It doesn't matter." Her mum said lamely, hovering anxiously, although Cassie knew that it *did* matter. Cassie's dad would be cross and grumpier than ever when Lorna went back, he hated being left sitting in the wheelchair half-dressed. Cassie fumbled with her bag for some minutes, seemingly unable to get the straps undone properly, so that she could open it and put the sandwich tub in. She was trying not to think about her sister, because she didn't want get to upset on the way to school, but already tears were pricking under her lower eyelids. She could not help thinking about Lizzie, especially today; she knew she wasn't supposed to think about her, because she couldn't stop crying then, but how could she help but remember? This was about the fifth time Cassie had forgotten her lunch this month. She had never forgotten anything when Lizzie had been there.

Lizzie was such a wonderful older sister, getting ready for school with Lizzie had never been a hardship, it was fun. Lizzie had made Cassie's morning routine into a terrific standing joke. Lizzie would stand by the front door, reeling off a list of things that needed to be in Cassie's bags before they left, and ticking off a pretend inventory of the various items Cassie needed for that day: packed lunch, every day, PE kit Tuesdays, Wednesdays, pencil case, every day, library book Thursdays... Cassie would run backwards and forwards collecting articles, as if she were taking part in a relay; even mum joined in, appearing at the kitchen door, immaculately dressed for the office and with one hand sorting her briefcase but still not too busy with the other to wave sandwich boxes or drinks containers. By the time the girls left for school, Cassie was breathless and laughing, but organised. Mum would be ready as well and all three would jump in the car together, 'Charlie's Angels' mum used to call them, then the girls were dropped off at the other school, the private school, on the far side of the town. *The school where all their friends were now.*

What a contrast to this morning. Cassie's eyes had begun to water even as she stood in the street fumbling uselessly at the straps on her bag. Lorna saw the tears and roughly snatched her daughter's bag and sandwich tub, with two swift movements she opened the bag and quickly shoved the lunch into it. Neither of them said anything about this, they both knew that it was just easier for Lorna to do it than wait for Cassie. As she zipped up the bag and put it on Cassie's shoulder, Lorna had started talking briskly in a gritted teeth, determined-to-be-cheerful type of manner.

"Go on now, you'll be late. Don't forget, be good at school and no daydreaming when you should be listening. Yes?"

"Yes, mum."

"You'll try really hard for me?"

"I promise." Lorna had smiled and patted Cassie's arm, then turned to hurry away.

"No making things up, either, stick to the truth and you won't go wrong," mum added, as she dashed home. Cassie bit her lip as she thought of her mum's last words; she knew that if she told the truth now Mrs Harrison was going to go barmy at her, but she had promised.

"Well, Miss Edwards, for the final time, *were you listening?*" Cassie kept her head down, she felt like she was going to be sick; the class waited expectantly, hopefully.

"No, Mrs Harrison I wasn't." She answered, and as Mrs Harrison went pale and clutched the side of her desk, the other children, led by Savannah, erupted into gales of laughter.

It was some minutes before Mrs Harrison regained her composure. Savannah anticipated the moment exactly, and nudged her neighbour warningly the second before Mrs Harrison shot a fierce warning look about the room, checking for troublemakers and silencing her students with one glare. As the children settled and became quiet the teacher walked angrily down the aisle and stood in front of Cassie's desk. She bent over, lowering her face so that it was just a breath away from that of her pupil's. The mingled smell of sweat and halitosis swept into Cassie's nostrils, making Cassie's nose twitch in distaste, so that Mrs Harrison now thought that the girl was making fun of her.

"Miss Edwards you are so hardened that you try my patience to the absolute limit. What kind of family life produces insolence like this?" The slight against her home was too much for Cassie and a sob escaped her. Mrs Harrison knew very little about Cassie's family, she had been off sick last year when Cassie had moved schools, just after the accident had happened. Mrs Harrison had been told, on her return, that there was something on Cassie's file about a car crash, but she hadn't had time to read any notes, and anyway these things were sadly becoming commonplace, one had to learn to move on, Mrs Harrison thought. Was it this pupil who had lost her father in an accident? She wasn't sure, but she spoke a little less harshly just in case.

"Your only redeeming feature is your honesty, but that is not enough. Come and stand at the front where I can see you." Cassie hastily brushed a tear away from her cheek and stood up obediently. Unfortunately for Cassie, but to the further amusement of the rest of the class, in her haste to obey Cassie had moved too quickly and she had forgotten to push her chair away first, before standing up. The light, easily unbalanced, plastic chair went flying backwards, clattering to the floor with a resounding echo. The class howled with laughter and Cassie's face flamed red, as she turned to stare at the chair, her hand vaguely flailing in its direction as if to belatedly catch it. Mrs Harrison stared at the back of Cassie's bent head, furious; she was convinced Cassandra had done this on purpose, probably because someone had told Cassandra that she, Mrs Harrison, was soft. At that moment Cassie nervously looked round to offer an apology to Mrs Harrison and attempted a smile, which only infuriated the teacher more.

"Are you smirking at me Cassandra?" She demanded furiously, her neck reddening into blotches with anger.

The class had noticed and were nudging each other, their initial burst of laughter, over the fall of the chair, had been quickly silenced and they were listening intently. Savannah was dying to giggle but even she dare not risk the wrath of Mrs Harrison in this mood, she was pleased to see that the teacher was practically choking on her words.

"I have had enough. Go and stand at the front of the class for the rest of the lesson, and make sure you wait to see me at the end!" Mrs Harrison followed Cassie back to the front and placed her standing adjacent to the desk, facing the class, within kicking distance of Savannah's sandals, before she delivered her final punishment.

"There will be a letter waiting for your, er," briefly her eyes flickered away, awkwardly, "er..mother." Cassie's eyes filled with water and her chin wobbled, Savannah was delighted, she was determined to make Cassie cry properly. As soon as Mrs Harrison had shaken her head despairingly at Cassie for one last time, and then turned back to begin writing on the black-board, Savannah carefully lifted her feet away from the ground, so that Mrs Harrison would not hear the tell-tale sound of movement as the soles of Savannah's shoes returned to touch the floor. Swinging her legs towards Cassie's ankles, she began kicking them, first one and then the other, in a constant rhythm. Savannah was disappointed, however, by the lack of satisfactory response, because even though Cassie flinched automat-ically as Savannah's shoe caught her bare ankles, she said nothing, nor did she even look in Savannah's direction. Savannah realised with frustration that Cassie was already off in her daft dream world again.

★ ★ ★

Cassie had not intended to begin daydreaming again so quickly. Standing by the teacher's desk, she had merely been trying to avoid locking eyes with any of the other children, especially that one right in front of her. Knowing that meeting just one look from Savannah would turn her insides into liquid, Cassie had quickly turned her attention to the pieces of work displayed on the classroom walls. She had skimmed over the neatest examples of handwriting and the smartest pieces of art work, when she caught sight of the postcards on the far wall. 'Holidays' a painted title announced. Cassie had been desperate to paint the title, and had managed to pluck up just enough nerve to ask, but Savannah had heard Cassie's request and said surely *she* should get to do it, as a reward for bringing in the most holiday post-cards. Mrs Harrison didn't think about the decision too long; Savannah's work was so neat, and Cassie's so variable, so Cassie had got the job of cutting out borders. She wasn't very good at that either and Savannah had promptly accused her of deliberate sabotage, but Mrs Harrison, when called to inspect by Savannah's loud complaints, merely shook her head and said "Oh dear, typical Cassie" which made Cassie feel stupid again, like she did most days at school. It was ridiculous really, when the others made it look so easy, but for Cassie it seemed impossible. She honestly felt that the scissors had a will of their own, and that their will was to go for a meandering zig-zaggy line up and down the paper, so that her neat line ended up looking like a fringe. It was a source of continual amazement to her, that the others could chatter and cast their gaze over all sorts of things when they were cutting out and *still* manage to produce a straight line, whereas she could never succeed at it, no matter how hard she tried. It even went wrong when she used a pencil and ruler to mark the place and then followed it with the scissors slowly and carefully, looking neither to the right nor the left, but only at the pencil mark, with such concentration that sometimes her tongue poked out from between her teeth with the effort. She hated it when her tongue slipped out like that, and of course Savannah always noticed it before everyone else and began name-calling. Usually it was just something uninspiring like 'stupid baby', but, once, Cassie's heart nearly stopped because she thought Savannah had called her *Lizzie Edwards*. She had paled, and Savannah had noticed immediately; with delight she had repeated her words:

"Cassie sticks her tongue out, let's name her Lizard Edwards." Savannah's friends had eagerly repeated it but Cassie had looked so relieved, in fact, almost pleased with the repetition, that Savannah had been disappointed, and even stopped commenting on the tongue for a while.

Cassie was glad to see that, from here, you couldn't see how messy the border was. In fact, from a distance it was quite effective and made the postcards really stand out; she soon spotted the one she had carefully brought in, the only one she had got from last year's family holiday. It was easy to spot as it was all black, except for three words which she knew by heart anyway, '*Skegness by night*'. Lizzie had chosen it, and they had laughed and laughed when they had picked it up in the shop. That was on the last day of their fantastic holiday. Cassie had loved every minute. There had been lots of swimming,

9

an adventure playground and, at night, a disco where dad had whirled mum around in their own version of dancing, while she and Lizzie pretended not to have anything to do with them. That had been the best of all, having Lizzie there. Lizzie to play with morning, noon and night, Lizzie thinking up games, Lizzie never complaining or even seeming to notice if Cassie was clumsy, or dropped something, or didn't like the noise of the other children and wanted to go somewhere else. People commented on the fact that they had got on together so well, it was rare, they said. Sometimes it was a small comfort to Cassie to think that she had appreciated her sister when she was alive. No one could have known what would happen within weeks of their return.

Looking at the postcard, oblivious to Mrs Harrison's words and the nudging of various elbows as people stared at her, Cassie was daydreaming again, reliving the minutes of that last ever family holiday. A huge tear rolled down her face and splashed to the floor. The class watched, fascinated, as one after another fell. While Mrs Harrison kept her back turned, to finish writing on the board, Savannah mimicked Cassie's tears, sliding a manicured finger down each of her smooth cheeks and flicking her fingers as each one fell. The gesture amused the children around her, but failed to make the slightest impression on Cassie; she stared past all the faces that swam before her, oblivious to Savannah and everyone. Seeing the postcard had made her think of last summer, and now Cassie was lost in dreams, remembering the time she had spent with her sister, terrified of forgetting anything about her.

Chapter 2

Cassie got home late that evening, but it seemed that no one had noticed. Her mum and dad were in their usual places, dad was sitting at one side of the table in the dining room, mum at the other. Dad's wheelchair was deliberately pushed right underneath the table, so that it was hidden from view by the table's broad surface and the other chairs. He was busy doing his matchstick model, and the daily routine was that Cassie always went up to him to enquire about progress. He would lay the matches down and point and explain, and Lorna would smile gratefully then get up and take herself off into the kitchen. Those few minutes when Cassie was listening to her dad gave Lorna a brief moment to herself, a precious respite where she wasn't being asked to pass things or to reach things or to move something. Mike was still trying to live as if nothing had changed, Lorna didn't blame him, but she found it hard that in his determination to carry on as normal, he asked Lorna to perform the most menial of tasks, rather than learn a new way to deal with them himself. Lorna never complained though, she smiled brightly, although her lips were tightly sealed and turned up at the edges only slightly.

When Cassie entered the dining room, her mum smiled the thin smile and got up to go into the kitchen.

"Just pass the paper, love?" Her dad said without looking up. The newspaper was at one end of the table and he was at the other; he could have reached it with a stick or something. Lorna leaned across the table and pushed the paper towards him, catching her stomach on the back of a chair; yet still she smiled grimly at Mike's bent head. Cassie hated that smile, it reminded her of one of those miserable looking clowns she'd seen once at an animal-free circus with Lizzie – they had worn huge red painted smiles, but they had not looked happy, most of them kept getting drenched with water or pretend custard pies. Cassie wanted to ask her mother why she didn't just tell her dad to get his paper himself, but Cassie never said the words out loud; she already knew the answer. She knew Lorna did not want to draw attention to Mike's difficulties. It was worse because he had been so independent, so active, before the accident. The awful thing was that *before* he would have laughed at the idea of a grown man sitting around, pretending he loved doing matchstick models; and now here he was, trying to convince everyone it was his life's work.

"Still," Lorna kept telling Cassie, "it is nice for you and dad to share an interest." Sometimes, Casssie wanted to say that she didn't really share the interest; that she only spoke to Dad because she felt her mum desperately needed her to. Besides, it wasn't strictly true, there was a small curiosity about what might have changed, and she did find it a little interesting to see the model take shape bit by bit, day by day; it was just that some days Cassie would much rather come home and slump in front of the TV, like she used to do with Lizzie. She sighed and her dad looked up.

"Oh, hi there. I didn't hear you come in." Lorna was about to go into the kitchen, and leave them to discussing which part had been added today, when she remembered her conversation with Cassie that morning.

"I think somebody might need a hug. How did it go?" Lorna was looking at Cassie with an intense hopeful expression, her blue eyes staring into Cassie's face. Cassie swallowed nervously; she could feel her eyelids starting to twitch already.

"Got you a letter." Cassie mumbled.

Disappointment silenced all three of them and Cassie's stomach churned, noisily, she thought, surely they could hear it . Her dad picked up a matchstick and started viciously rubbing it, before he muttered bitterly.

"How many is that, now? Four this month?"

"Mike." Lorna said warningly, then she turned to Cassie and there was that awful, clown-smile on her lips.

"Now Cassie, do you want to give us the letter and then perhaps we'll talk about it later, when Dad and I have had a chance to look over it?" Cassie nodded dumbly and handed it over to her mother. She looked across at her father but Mike would not look at her, he was filing a match away to nothing, and grumbling under his breath about the quality of the wood.

"Dad?" Cassie ventured nervously.

"Go tidy that midden if you want something to do," he suggested.

"Midden?" Cassie asked, tears welling up in her eyes.

"That heap of rubbish you call your bedroom. Your mum nearly broke her ankle this morning, when she tried to get in to put some of your clothes in the wardrobe." Cassie looked at her mum worriedly and Lorna shook her head sadly.

"I'm sorry, Cassie, but it is a bit of a problem. I can help you later if you like..." Lorna began, but Mike interrupted her.

"She's big enough to do it herself, Lorna, it's no use us doing it for her, mollycoddling! Won't do her any good in the long run." Lorna stared at Mike, and for a brief instant anger replaced the pity in her expression as she considered his words. '*Mollycoddling*?' What did he think she was doing with him? She was going to speak, until she looked at his bent, miserable shoulders and found that she could say nothing. She turned her gaze helplessly to her daughter. Cassie's eyes were huge bubbles of tears now; Lorna couldn't bear to look at them.

"Go do your room now, and I'll call you down when dinner's ready."

★　★　★

Cassie always had difficulty keeping her bedroom tidy, even though it was the smallest room in the house. Lizzie had done her best to help, she'd turned boring tidying up into an exciting Treasure Hunt of lost and forgotten things; dolls which turned up under the bed became kidnapped Princesses that Cassie had rescued and returned to their homes in the doll's house, a hunt for overdue library books was turned into the search for the Holy Grail; Cassie and Lizzie followed the trail to get to them using the secret instructions of 'where did I have it last?' and the ultimate Enigma style code-breaker of 'what did I do with it then?' Those were the days when you could still see the floor. Cassie sighed heavily, and bent down to pick up one of her and Lizzie's Jacqueline Wilson books. Someone had brought them a set to share the Christmas before last. They had joked about how to divide them when they had grown up and left home, Cassie had said Lizzie could have them all, as

Lizzie was the better reader, but Lizzie had said that meant Cassie should have them as she needed the practice! They never settled it. Cassie supposed they were all hers now; the thought gave her no pleasure. She lifted up 'Bad Girls' to put it back on the bookcase. As soon as she touched it, the pages opened onto a particularly interesting part: poor bullied Mandy was finally having some fun and going with her new friend Tanya for a swimming session. There were two pictures on this part, which made it a bit easier for her to read. The book reminded her of Lizzie, who had read it to her one night when neither of them could get to sleep. Cassie didn't remember looking at it since, she had no idea how it had come out of the bookcase and ending up on the floor. Sitting down in the midst of the disorder, she looked at the pictures first and then tried to read. At first the words shifted a little, as if settling themselves down into place, and then she had to rub her eyes which had begun itching and watering. They often did when she had to look closely at printed text. Soon she began to recognise words and remember Lizzie reading them, she could hear the intonations of Lizzie's voice and even the bits where they had both laughed. Suddenly, it was much easier to read; easier than she had ever found it before. Gradually she became absorbed and began turning the pages, leaning back casually she managed to squash one side of a jigsaw box without even being aware of its presence.

An hour later her mother's voice called up the stairs, "Cassie, tea's ready!" and then, sighing, repeated it again after five minutes. Cassie heard her the third time and looked about her in surprise. Realising that she must go down she put the book back on the shelf and sailed down the stairs humming a tune and only when she walked into the dining room and saw her parent's faces did she remember the letter.

"Sit down love, eat your tea while it's warm," Lorna smiled cheerfully at her daughter and Cassie's heart sank; she was going to get a 'pep talk'.

"Thanks, Mum. Lasagne, delicious!" She smiled widely, hoping to deflect the coming lecture. It worked, briefly, Lorna smiled again; more genuinely this time.

"Well its nice to get a bit of appreciation now and again, thank you Cassie." She turned to Mike and gave him a look which said clearly 'well she may be struggling at school but at least she has manners' and then they all ate their meal in companionable silence. Afterwards, Cassie remembered to take her plate into the kitchen, and was just about to sneak out of the door to go back upstairs when the summons came.

"Cassie, love, your dad and I would like a word with you." Cassie stopped, her shoulders drooped and she frowned. She turned to face her parents and keeping her eyes down, slid into a chair between them.

"Yes?" she asked sadly, her finger lazily tracing the whorled pattern of the wood in the scratched surface of the table. The soft pine still glowed, oblivious to the scars of etched pen; its battered appearance never detracted from the friendly warmth. Cassie remembered very well how she and her sister had climbed on it when they were young, to shine the surface by sliding up and down with their woolly tights on. Lorna had laughed and laughed until the tears had rolled down her face and had not even told them to get down. In fact, after that, she had always let them 'polish' the table their way. Cassie wondered if her mum ever thought about it. The table was squirted with Mr Sheen now, it didn't shine half as much. There wasn't so much laughter, either, Cassie could understand that though, they all missed Lizzie so much. Cassie's head drooped further and a tear dropped down, her mother saw it and quickly picked up Cassie's hand in her own, but Lorna's fingers were colder than the table.

"Cassie, darling, don't worry. We didn't think the letter was that bad. Mrs Harrison mentioned insolence, I know, but we were waiting to hear your side first, of course." Her mother was being kind, and even her father awkwardly pushed his arm across her shoulders.

"Come on, love, it's okay." He murmured.

"We won't talk about it if it's upsetting." Her mother decided, hurriedly talking as she watched a second tear slowly sliding down Cassie's cheek; Lorna's voice had become panicky, as it always did when Cassie started to get emotional.

"You've only got another few weeks left in Mrs Harrison's class anyway, so then you'll have a fresh start." Cassie opened her mouth to speak, she wanted to say that it wasn't school, or at least, not just that. She lifted her head to begin and her eyes met those of her mother. Immediately Lorna became even more frantic, it was as if she knew what Cassie was going to say; she dropped Cassie's hand and pressed her own hands together deliberately.

"Enough tears!" she pronounced fiercely, "School's not worth all this upset. Let's talk about something nice." Mike looked across, surprised at her sudden change in tone, he looked as if he was about to protest but when he caught sight of Lorna's face he gulped back the words and turned to look out of the window, swallowing hard. Lorna carried on, forcing herself to be cheerful; her voice came out in a strangulated rapid torrent.

"Now let's see, something good to talk about. Isn't it your school trip next week? I loved school trips when I was your age. Didn't it say on the form I sent back that you were going to Howarth?" She challenged, her eyes peering wildly into Cassie's, desperate for an attempt at normality. Cassie nodded dumbly, she couldn't bring herself to speak, but her mother was satisfied. Mike turned his head bleakly towards them.

"Howarth, eh?" he murmured. "Hmm." Lorna flashed him a plaintive look, 'please make the effort' her eyes begged. She was desperate to prevent silence and went on talking quickly, rambling really.

"I remember going to Howarth, what a lovely place, I went when I was at school."

"Did you?" Mike asked, his brow twitching as he struggled to think of something to add. "Erm, do you know, I think someone famous lived there once." Lorna nodded at him gratefully, Cassie's tears had stopped, she was looking at her parents and listening,

"Yeah, erm, let me think." Mike said, "Who was it? Guess before I count to five!" He challenged Cassie suddenly; Cassie was shocked, but immediately began thinking hard, she rubbed her cheek with the back of her hand to clear her wet skin. It was an automatic gesture, not one seeking attention. Cassie had forgotten about her tears, she was frowning in concentration.

"One... Two..." Mike was speaking slowly, and quietly, anxiously studying his daughter's expression, carefully monitoring his counting so that Cassie would have just long enough, and no more. Lorna's face lost some of its tension. She knew the answer to the question, she was sure that Mike did too. This was one of the games he had always played with Lizzie.

"Three... Four... Four and a half..."

"Stop!" Cassie suddenly called out triumphantly, "I know! It was the Brontës!"

"Yeah, you got me! You win!" Mike said, smiling.

"There were a few of them weren't there?" Lorna interjected. "All famous writers? Except one, but I'm not sure which. I think we might have visited their house on our trip. Didn't they live in a vicarage?"

"The Parsonage, Mum, That's where we're going, we're doing about the Brontës." Cassie said with enthusiasm, excited, but still with a rather anxious tone to her voice.

"Course you are, silly me." Lorna said with relief; she was happier now that she had got Cassie to think about something else, but what had been on Cassie's mind still lay between them, and they were all consciously trying to put on a brave face.

"It must be the same place that I went to." Lorna continued, her voice wavering less and less, her speech slowing, and becoming more relaxed. "It was very historical anyway, and if I remember rightly it was supposed to be kept just as it was in the Brontës' time. Some of their clothes were still in the rooms, I think. I remember we all were amazed by this really small dress, would fit you probably, Cass, and yet it belonged to one of the grown ups. There was other stuff too, furniture and things. Apparently it hadn't changed in over a hundred years."

"Watch out for the toilets, then!" Mike put in, forcing his face into an ugly grimace; his expression was so hideous that it elicited a giggle from Cassie.

"Trust you to lower the tone!" Lorna mock scolded, but she laughed as well, evidently relieved. Cassie took this as her cue,

"Can I go now mum?" she asked politely, "I've got something I'm busy with in my bedroom."

"As long as you've done your homework then," her mum bargained, "I don't want another note tomorrow." Cassie nodded, her cheeks flaming with the remembrance, and left her parents sitting there silently. Lorna had turned to stare out of the window, her face, hidden from view, had dropped its false smile, but Cassie would not have preferred the reality. Lorna was a picture of misery, her mouth hung slackly, both ends curved down cutting deep grooves on each side of her chin, her brow heavy over her eyes, lines furrowed her forehead. She was evidently exhausted by her attempts at animation; her hand slid across the table in the direction of Cassie's departure, unconsciously following the same path as Cassie's had done, until it paused over one of the thick, swirling knots in the golden surface. Lorna's eyes were deliberately turned to look out of the window, and she held her right hand to the side of her face so that it appeared she was only resting her face on her hand, when in fact she was purposely shielding her expression from Mike's inquisitive eyes. The pose was unnecessary: Mike had picked up several of his matches and held them close to his face, concentrating his whole attention on pushing together the thin splinters of wood. Neither of them spoke, they just sat there in silence. Lorna slid her hand very slowly over the surface of the whorl, indiscernible to the touch. The sensitive tips of her fingers felt only the flattened pine, the wood had been carefully manufactured to be as smooth as possible. All of her senses were oblivious to the twisting tumult of knots within.

Chapter 3

At school the next day, Cassie tried really hard to concentrate. Mrs Harrison was talking about the trip, enthusiastically explaining about the Brontë Sisters, who had, as she was sure they all knew, *because she had already told them,* become famous published writers as adults. She wanted to impress upon them the fact that the sisters had begun their careers when they were the same age as the children in the class were now,

"By making their own little home-made books. Isn't that amazing?"

"They must have had a boring life, Miss" said Jason, "I never look at books, I'm far too busy on my Playstation."

"Yeah Miss, books are for girls, I bet if it was the Brontë Brothers they wouldn't have been making sissy books."

"There was a boy, Matthew." Mrs Harrison corrected. "His name was Branwell and he wrote just as much as the girls, possibly more."

"Yeah an' I bet his books are more famous now aren't they?" Tim taunted, trying to irritate those pupils who were listening entranced.

"Not at all. Not one of Branwell's books was published. Several poems were though, but the point is that *all* the children were writing at the age you are now. It wasn't easy for them, paper was an expensive luxury in those times, they were living in the midst of dreadful poverty such as you and I would find difficult to imagine. Yet they made these books."

"So they weren't that poor then, Miss" sneered Brian, "Not if they had all that paper."

"I was just getting to that, thank you Brian, but at least it shows you were taking an interest and listening so *well done*." At this unlikely admonishment, Brian looked aghast and several of the boys sniggered. Brian frequently aimed his sarcasm at the teachers, in order to ingratiate himself with the in-crowd, especially Jason, who found him irritating in the extreme and had started off the laughter at Mrs Harrison's reply. Cassie remained silent during all this, and hoped that Mrs Harrison would notice her efforts at concentration, but no comment was made.

"Now then class, Brian has raised an interesting point, can anyone tell me what books are made of?" The children looked about each other, puzzled by the obviousness of the answer, but one or two hands went slowly up, Mrs Harrison pointed at each in turn.

"Yes, Natasha?"

"Paper, Miss"

"Yes, that's probably the main thing isn't it, what else?"

"Cardboard, Miss"

"Yes, anything more unusual perhaps?" There was a pause, then hands appeared again.

"My baby sister's got one made out of plastic Mrs Harrison, it floats in the bath."

"Miss, I've got one made out of cloth, my Nan gave it to me, she had it when she was little."

"That might be interesting to bring in, Sophie if your Nan doesn't mind."

"It doesn't matter Miss, she's dead." Sophie said bluntly, silencing Mrs Harrison temporarily, while the teacher quickly decided how to react to the statement. Mrs Harrison did not want to cause further upset to a newly bereaved pupil, but it was clear that in this case she need not have worried. Sophie was extremely blasé about the whole thing, and at that moment was eagerly looking round for a response: she was not disappointed, there was a burst of sniggering, but Cassie had gone white and was clearly uncomfortable. Several of the children began nudging each other, Savannah bent to whisper something to Poppy, and the class quickly became restless. Mrs Harrison, noticing, called out briskly.

"Any more ideas?"

"Miss, Mrs Harrison, my Gran's got a talking book from the blind people."

"Miss I've got a talking book, it's got Mickey Mouse on it!" There was laughter, and Mrs Harrison smiled.

"Well that woke you all up. Now then, back to the Brontë children, I won't say the Brontë Sisters because it would be a shame to miss out Branwell, as he was a very enthusiastic contributor to the books. In fact, it was his idea for the Brontë children to produce a magazine of their own, based on their favourite journal, 'Blackwood's Magazine.'"

"Yeah, Miss, see, the boy had the best ideas." Brian shouted out. Mrs Harrison glared at his interruption, but replied calmly.

"Yes, Brian, it was a good idea."

"Boys have got the best ideas, miss, and the best imagination, Miss." Brian called out again. Mrs Harrison sighed.

"We're not getting into the battle of the sexes, Brian," she began, raising her eyebrows at the giggles that went round the class at her use of the word 'sexes'. "Suffice to say that *all* the Brontë children had very good imaginations, although on the day Branwell named the magazine his must have had a day off, as the title of the new creation was merely "Branwell's Blackwood's Magazine." A titter went round the class, several of the children began to suggest their own alternatives.

"Brian's Boring Magazine."

"Savannah's super School Magazine." Said one of the acolytes, Poppy, Cassie thought. Another, Sophie, sneered.

"No, 'Savvy's Savvy magazine.'" She looked across to Savannah for approval but Savannah was about to speak.

"Cassie's Clumsy Magazine." A voice rang out clearly, Cassie's eyes filled and she bit her lip. Mrs Harrison glared at Poppy, although Cassie was sure it was *Savannah*'s voice; certainly Poppy's wasn't usually so loud.

"Very imaginative, Poppy." Mrs Harrison said curtly. "*If* I can continue now. The Brontë children did use some paper for their work, and for their covers they used all sorts of materials: bits of sugar bags, scraps of wallpaper, whatever they could find."

"Did you say bits of sugar bags, miss?"

"Yes I did, Natasha. Do you think you could use something like that? "

"Crisp packets maybe."

"Yeah Miss we could have the Quavers Quiz Book."

"Well, I'm glad you are applying what you have learnt in class to your own experience, but actually modern day crisp packets are many times bigger than the little books the Brontës made. As I said, paper was very expensive, so the books they wrote had to be very small, not much bigger than a matchbox,

"But Miss, if they were that small, how could they write them, the pen would be too big."

"They didn't even have pens, not that you would recognise. They had quill pens though."

"Miss, what's a quill pen?"

"A feather, specially sharpened and ink goes in the hollow spine in the middle. That would be fun for you all wouldn't it? Think of the mess you could make with that, you'd have ink all over the place! Schools were *very strict* in those days about being neat, which some of you here would find very difficult!" Mrs Harrison paused and allowed herself a few moments to look specifically at a number of children, for whom her remarks were particularly pertinent. Mainly it was the boys, but she aimed a long look in Cassie's direction. Cassie fidgeted uncomfortably; she knew her hand writing was a mess, try as she might there was nothing she could do to alter it. Her parents had spent hours practising with her, buying handwriting activity books with page after page of lines to trace and copy. The pages were babyish, the sort you gave to a toddler who'd just learnt to hold a pencil, but Cassie had forced herself to practise. It was all to no avail. As soon as she got the pen in her hand and began to write, her eyes could only watch helplessly as the scrawl appeared. She willed the letters to go on to the page, but her fingers seemed to have a mind of their own, and the lines would spider off all over the paper, so that even she couldn't read her own finished work.

Mrs Harrison had finished her perusal of the class and

resumed her lecture.

"The Brontës were not alone in their need to write as much as possible on a limited amount of paper. It was common practice in those days for people to write the first side of a letter, and then, instead of turning the piece of paper *over* they turned the page round, on its side, and wrote across the lines or upside down, between them."

"Is that what it means when people say "reading between the lines", Miss?" Savannah called out confidently, in the same clear tones of the voice that had just been attributed to Poppy.

"That could be where the term originated, Savannah, dear." the teacher nodded, smiling, "And of course, if you had to economise on paper, you could always do as the Brontës did, and write very, very small, minuscule, in fact."

"Miss," Ryan shouted eagerly, cleverly mimicking Savannah, "Is that what it means when we have a school for minis?" The class tittered and in the ensuing mayhem, Cassie finally found courage to put her hand up. Mrs Harrison noticed the gesture and raised her eyebrows reluctantly, nodding in Cassie's direction.

"Miss, how could they read the books if the writing was so small?"

"That's an interesting question Cassandra, well done. The writing is very tiny, we would certainly need a magnifying glass to read it, but I don't know whether they had one or not; perhaps you could keep an eye out for one at the museum tomorrow?" She actually smiled at Cassie and Cassie felt a warm glow of pleasure, she smiled back at Mrs Harrison, until she realised that Savannah's gaze was fixed upon her, as cold, calculating and hungry as a snake fixes on its prey.

Chapter 4

The day of the trip dawned, and Cassie was awoken by her mum bringing in her morning cup of tea. As Cassie wriggled to sit up, Lorna sat down at the edge of her bed smiling and passed the mug,

"Watch your fingers, it's hot."

"Well I don't want it if it's cold!" Cassie joked cheekily.

"It's nice to see you so perky this morning," Lorna remarked, "I bet it's because it's your trip, no work, all play, all day!"

"Are you saying I'm lazy?" Cassie asked quickly, her eyes large and liquid already.

"You're far too sensitive for your own good." Her mother replied impatiently, getting up, "You know I was teasing, well you should do. Anyway, it's time to get dressed and tell me what you want in your packed lunch."

"Okay, mum." Cassie replied, subdued, and leaned back against the headboard, spilling some of the tea on the duvet cover. She hastily wiped it as her mum pulled open the curtains and the sun rushed in, flooding the room with warm yellow light. Unfortunately, Lorna turned and noticed the giveaway motion of her daughter's hand on the cover.

"Oh, Cassie." She said wearily. "Is it soaked? Will I have to wash it? I've just filled the washer with sheets and pyjamas, your dad's..." Lorna stopped guiltily; she knew Mike would be devastated if she carried on.

Luckily Cassie hadn't realised, she was still checking the quilt cover.

"It doesn't look too bad, mum, it's just that the sun was so bright, it shocked me!" Cassie's mum looked at her quickly, and bent down to examine it for herself.

"It'll do, thank goodness." She said, looking out of the window. "I suppose the sun is quite dazzling," she conceded, adding brightly, "All the glory of Heaven, just for your school trip."

"A normal person would just say it's a sunny day." Cassie remarked, trying to make her mum smile, but her mum took it the wrong way. She didn't say anything, she just bit her lip and looked in Cassie's direction with a wounded look, making Cassie feel mean.

"Sorry, mum, I didn't mean...."

"Forget it, Cass." Her mum interrupted, disappearing out of the room before Cassie got the chance to say anything else. "It's time to get ready anyway." She shouted back, drowning Cassie's final 'but Mum.' Cassie sat there, morosely finishing her tea, and thought about what Mrs Harrison had said about the Brontës. Their dad had been the vicar. I wonder if they ever got sick of their dad's religion. Of course she guessed why Lorna had started hovering around churches, but Lorna never discussed it with her, or invited her to come; she was secretive, Cassie thought she was terrified of being cast as a 'religious freak'. 'And now I've walked straight into it.' Cassie scolded herself, 'God, I'm stupid.'

★   ★   ★

When Cassie got to school that morning, the coach was waiting and the children were busily pairing up to sit together. Cassie noticed immediately that most of the girls were already possessively clutching a partner, standing guard over rucksacks stuffed with food and waterproofs, and cosily chatting. She assumed that they had arranged this that day after class, when she had had to stay behind and talk to Mrs Harrison. Savannah stood in her designer label matching jacket and rucksack, making a good pretence of chattering happily to Poppy, but all the time carefully watching Cassie as she walked across the playground and joined the group standing by the coach. When Cassie's eyes finally dared to look in Savannah's direction, a small smile of triumph appeared on Savannah's face and she turned to say something to Poppy, but Poppy had turned to talk to another girl on her other side, and wasn't paying any attention to Savannah. Savannah was furious, and nudged Poppy viciously. Poppy yelped and turned round quickly, mouth open in a round 'O' of complaint. At first Cassie thought Poppy was actually going to protest to Savannah, but when Poppy saw the expression on Savannah's face, her eyes looked frightened, and she dropped her gaze. Savannah was satisfied and leaned over to whisper something, pointing in Cassie's direction. Poppy dutifully looked over, but although she nodded, and tried to smile at Savannah's words, she flushed uncomfortably. Savannah turned to Cassie and saw her watching, and suddenly started laughing very loudly, staring at Cassie the whole time. She nudged Poppy again, and Poppy forced herself to laugh too, but it was rather false, and she couldn't look Cassie in the eye. Jason heard the sound of laughter and turned round hopefully, but seeing nothing amusing, quickly turned back to his group, ignoring Savannah's slight bending of her fingers, in what she thought was a cool way to wave.

"Something amusing, Savannah?" Mr Field, the other teacher who would be accompanying them on the trip, asked pertinently. Savannah hadn't noticed him appear from behind the coach.

"Er, no, sir." She muttered, flustered out of her customary calm and composure. She had never been keen on Mr Field at the best of times, because when she was doing her best to be attentive and charming, the *image* of a perfect pupil, which worked so well on Mrs Harrison, Mr Field mimicked her smile exactly, looking for all the world as if he were sincere, while making comments about Savannah's impressive acting and future Oscar nominations that made the boys laugh.

"Quite sure, Savannah? We'll keep it that way, eh? Now show me how the model pupil gets on the coach, or do we need a photographer from the newspaper to take a snap? You seem to be in rather often, we don't want to miss an opportunity do we?" He was grinning when he said it and she walked up the stairs to the sound of Jason's group laughing. Savannah was furious, she blamed it on Cassie that Mr Field had noticed her. Savannah hoped that Cassie would be sitting across the aisle, so that she could amuse herself by kicking her legs all the way to Howarth. The children were getting on in pairs, having been told to sit with their partners. Poppy sat down next to her partner with some trepidation, but Savannah merely swung her legs to one side as she squeezed past.

"I need to sit in the aisle seat." She said gruffly, and then ignored Poppy. Poppy was relieved, she liked to look out of the window, and wouldn't have dared to ask to sit in the window seat. She was disappointed, though, because now it was clear that Savannah wanted to sit in silence, she didn't have anyone to talk to. She could hear the lively chatter of the two girls behind her, they sounded as if they were having much more fun. Still, she contented herself with thinking, it was something special to be the chosen best friend of the most popular girl in the class.

★　★　★

"Come along Cassandra, get your partner and hop onto the coach, we don't want to be late, do we?"

"But Sir, I haven't got a partner, there's no one left." Mr Field looked at her, exasperated, thinking to himself 'there's always one', but saying nothing out loud. He quickly scanned the playground and then the road outside at the last few stragglers coming late to school. His face changed as he recognised a small girl battling with a particularly large bag. Mr Field allowed himself a wry smile at the size of the bag, some parents packed for a day-trip as if their children would be away for a week.

"Ah, look, Laura Waterson, she's in your class. Now, you two pair up then, another problem solved!" He nodded at them vaguely, as he ushered both onto the coach. Laura looked up shyly at Cassie, she had joined the school only a few weeks ago and was the smallest child in the class. For most of the time since her arrival she had been mute, only once had Cassie ever heard her speak, and that was a desperate request for permission to go to the toilet, which Mrs Harrison had reluctantly given but only because everyone could see the anguished look on Laura's face. "Normally you should go in your break time," the teacher had replied to the air, as Laura had shot out of the classroom as if her desk had been on fire.

It looked like being a quiet journey to Howarth, Cassie thought, rather relieved, as both girls climbed onto the coach together. They squeezed down the narrow gap between the rows, towards one of the few pairs of seats left. Cassie struggled down the aisle with her bag, not noticing Savannah lying in wait, just behind the next set of chairs. She heard a cry, and turned to see Laura jammed behind her large bag, which was stuck between two seats. As she turned round to offer assistance, Savannah leaned out from her aisle seat and gave Cassie's bag, hanging heavily from one arm, a shove, so that it swung towards one of the pupils seated on the opposite side of the coach to Savannah. As Cassie realised, and twisted round to try to stop it from hitting the girl, Savannah's foot slid out in front of Cassie's ankle and she was knocked off balance. Cassie went flying down the aisle, her bag hitting the girl anyway, and also catching someone else's head on the way past. She fell heavily onto Laura's bag; freeing it, but almost knocking Laura back down the steps. Luckily Mr Field was just coming up on to the coach and he caught her easily.

"Enjoy your trip, ladies?" He joked. "Now then, it's a good job Laura's so light, are you both alright? How did that happen?" he asked, looking up the bus for tell tale shoes sticking out, or smirking faces, but the whole class was giggling, so it was difficult to tell.

"Laura was stuck, sir." Cassie mumbled by way of explanation.

"But clumsy Cassie tried to help!" A voice rang out from behind a chair, followed by more laughter. Mr Field wasn't sure whose it was, so he decided to ignore it; he looked at Cassie's hot embarrassed face and felt a rush of pity. He was glad Mrs Harrison hadn't seen, she was continually complaining about Cassie's clumsiness and insolence in the staff room at break. The teachers had begun to feel sorry for her, despite the fact that they all agreed she was a disaster area.

"So you decided to help? Well she's certainly not stuck now, so you must have succeeded, well done. Go and sit down now, it's nearly time to go, just waiting for Mrs Harrison." Cassie looked up in surprise, she had been expecting to be told off, or at least receive some form of dismissive comment, but he smiled at her and waved his hand in the direction of the last two empty seats. Mr Field remained standing at the front of the bus, in full view of all the pupils, and watched Cassie and Laura go safely up the aisle, before turning round and going back down the steps again; he wasn't sure which girl was the target or whether it had been genuine clumsiness that caused the incident, but he was experienced enough to know that there was more to gain from standing there visibly, than asking questions and trying to find out. Savannah saw him there and was staring at him, under the guise of opening the top of her bag to check her sandwiches; she had watched Cassie approach and had been forced to let her go past without a repetition of the foot movement, but she contented herself with sharply poking Cassie just above her hip. It was slyly done, as Savannah pretended to lean across to talk to the girl on the other side of the aisle, so that the gesture remained unseen even by the observant Mr Field. Cassie felt the prod but didn't bother reacting, she followed Laura to the empty seats and stopped, both girls sighed in unison.

"Over the wheels." Cassie guessed, looking at the raised curve beneath their feet,

"You're over the engine, you'll be sick." Jason chanted

34

behind them from the back row; Matthew and the rest of the gang joined in with vigour, Brian aiming to be the loudest. Savannah turned round just as the boys reached the crescendo of "Over the engine, you'll be sick." In their brief pause for breath, she stood up and turned round so that she was facing Cassie, one hand on her hip and the other tapping the side of her head meaningfully, and said tauntingly.

"Or are you sick already?" Cassie and Laura looked at each other but said nothing; Savannah had switched her gaze to meet Jason's, looking for approval. He grinned at her, then seeing a movement at the front of the bus silenced his gang with one swift arm movement just as Brian increased his volume even more. In the sudden cessation by the others, Brian Bottomley's lone voice shrilled out in high whiney tones down the coach.

"OVER THE ENGINE, YOU'LL BE SICK."

"Quiet at the back!" Mr Field roared from the step at the front of the bus.

"Yeah, quiet Brian!" echoed Jason, and he and the rest of the gang burst out into hearty laughter, much to Brian's dismay. Mr Field glared at them, then turned to talk to the driver. The vehicle was started and the floor began to vibrate beneath the girls' feet. They had to wait then while Mr Field discussed arrival times and plans with Mrs Harrison, and all the time the constant joggling of the engine rocked the seats. The smell of fumes began to slip in through the air vents over the children's heads. Several of the boys began fiddling and twisting them, but it was difficult to tell whether they had opened the vents or closed them. The rocking motion and the smell was making Cassie feel sick, just as she began to feel she could stand it no more, they finally set off.

The clouds clung close to the hills as the coach lumbered along the winding roads. It had been bright sunshine as they left the school, but the day had grown dull as soon as they had reached the outskirts of town. The valleys they passed through all looked the same to Cassie. The landscape was full of dark, Yorkshire mill towns, defiantly ugly with their blackened stone, staunchly supported by the earthy green and brown of the surrounding fields. Even in July, the outlook was bleak, Cassie thought, and shivered suddenly, prompting Laura into speech.

"You cold, Cassie?" she asked, her small face peering into Cassie's.

"No." Cassie replied without thinking, absorbed in the view from the window, "Someone stepped on my grave." The silence that followed the remark drew Cassie's attention and she felt uneasy when she realised what she had said. It was something she and Lizzie had said often, never considering what it might mean. Laura continued to look at her oddly, Cassie felt like an idiot.

"It's just a stupid saying, Laura, you must have heard of it!" She asked, and watched with relief as Laura's face cleared.

"No I haven't heard of it, is it a Yorkshire saying?" Laura asked timidly; she had moved from the South and had found the change in accents and use of language confusing at first.

"I don't know, I assumed everyone knew it," Cassie replied, puzzled.

There was a silence; neither girl knew what to say. Cassie resumed looking out of the window, they were nearly at Howarth, slowly shuddering down a hill, leading a straggling band of cars and vans. The drivers following kept nudging closer, each metre gained forcing them into closer mimicry of the coach's movements. Cassie could hear the boys on the back seat, jeering at the irritated drivers of the vehicles behind, but not loud enough for Mr Field to hear. She guessed they were making signs too, from the frequent, suppressed snorts and giggles.

"They all died you know," Laura blurted out suddenly.

"What? Who did?" Cassie asked, looking round at the boys quickly, just in case. Savannah was smiling at Jason, but he and the others were taking it turns to watch the front of the coach for Mr Field, then swivelling back to leer out of the window and annoy the drivers further; they all looked perfectly well.

"The Brontë children, the ones we're learning about, they all died quite young, my mum said so." Cassie looked at Laura, she seemed unperturbed, Cassie didn't know whether to laugh, was it a joke? Was she making some sort of sick reference to Lizzie?

"Well of course they died, it was a long time ago." Cassie replied curtly, and turned away. Unfortunately, because of the way Savannah had twisted round on her seat to see Jason, when Cassie faced into the aisle she had to stare right at Savannah and she knew Savannah would definitely notice. Savannah did notice, straight-away, she looked immediately at Cassie and her eyes were keenly speculative. Cassie quickly turned back to Laura and met that peculiar gaze, curious but uncritical. Laura stared at Cassie for a long time, until Cassie was quite uncomfortable, but then, without warning, Laura suddenly started talking again, very quickly and nervously, so that Cassie could barely figure out what she meant, and then, when she did realise, she wished she hadn't understood.

"You were quite interested yesterday weren't you? I noticed you were really listening to Mrs Harrison. That's not like you, is it?" Cassie was annoyed by the last phrase.

"What do you mean?" she enquired irritably.

"Don't worry, I wouldn't tell, but I know you're always staring out of the window." Laura carried on, looking more and more anxious as she spoke, but seemingly unable to stop the torrent of words once she had started despite Cassie's increasingly furrowed forehead.

"It's unnerving because I'm sat next to it, aren't I?" she waited for Cassie to agree, but Cassie had no idea where Laura was seated in the classroom and gave no response. Unperturbed, Laura carried on regardless.

"Well, loads of times I have to look past you to see Mrs Harrison and when I do it's like you're looking *right at me* and I smile, but you just blank me totally, as if you can see through me, like, I'm *invisible*." After her astonishingly long outburst, Laura paused to draw breath, her eyes still fixed on Cassie's face. She felt awful, but now she had finally spoken to someone, it seemed impossible to stop, so she carried on again before Cassie had chance to say anything.

"It's freaky, but then I realise you're daydreaming. When Mrs Harrison sees you, then she gets really narked, so I've tried to warn you sometimes, waving at you or pointing, but you never notice, it's so weird."

"Oh." Was all Cassie could manage in reply; she dropped her gaze and stared, seemingly transfixed, at her fingers, which were twisting unconsciously in her lap; she felt really stupid now.

"Perhaps I shouldn't have said anything." Laura said, finally drawing to a close. "To be honest, I don't know why I did, I don't normally talk to anyone and the first time I try I keep putting my foot in it! Forget I said anything, right? Silly Laura! Silly, silly Laura!" Laura was so cross at herself that she sounded quite funny. Cassie lifted her head slowly and stared at Laura's face, now turned out of the window, close to tears, she was biting her bottom lip. Cassie felt sorry for her, she stretched out an arm tentatively and tugged Laura's sleeve to get her attention. Laura turned round, still anxious.

"I'm sorry," Cassie began slowly. "I didn't know about the daydreaming, I mean, I know I *do* it, because Mrs Harrison tells me off, but I don't know I'm doing it when I'm actually doing it, if you see what I mean." It sounded confusing even to Cassie's ears, but it was not something she'd ever talked about with anyone.

"You must think I'm a right wierdo." She felt distinctly uncomfortable, and tears were pricking at her eyes, so she bent down to her bag to search for a tissue. Watching her fumbling about without success, Laura guessed what she was looking for, and started to tug a wad of paper handkerchiefs out of her pocket.

"My mum loaded me up this morning," she grinned, as she pulled, but the sheer number of them had caused them to jam on her pocket flap. "She's a bit obsessed about me never leaving home without a bag full of things that I won't need, and a tree's worth of tissues stuffed in my pocket." She gave the bundle a final pull and paper handkerchiefs flew everywhere. The girls gazed at the heap of white, scrunched handkerchiefs scattered all over their knees, the seat and the floor.

"Almost like a magician, pulling them out like that." Cassie muttered and then began to giggle. Cassie bent to help Laura pick them up, they both started laughing and the awkward feeling went. At that moment Mr Field happened to glance up the coach to check the boys, hearing laughter and seeing the girls giggling, he congratulated himself on seating them together.

Chapter 5

The coach finally pulled up in a dreary car park, deliberately buried behind houses. Mr Field insisted the class wait on board, until he and Mrs Harrison had checked with the museum that they were allowed to go in straightaway. The vehicle was hot and smelly now, in the dull humidity of the weather, and the view from the coach windows was of uninspiring back yards. Jason and his cronies on the back row, had spotted a resident who was regarding the schoolchildren disdainfully, and they were living up to expectations by gestures and grimaces.

"We ought to moon him," said Jason, looking round quickly, "Come on Brian you're nearest."

Brian went red and Savannah squealed with delight, so that all eyes turned to see what was going on.

"Don't be daft, Jase," Brian spluttered. "He can see we're from a school, what if he rings the coach company?" Jason was irritated by the logical reasoning of Brian's refusal, but quickly dismissed it.

"Nah, only a bonehead would do that, someone like you. You know what you are, you're a chicken!"

"Chicken."

The boys around Jason started to chant and Brian looked wildly about at them, desperate for escape but the mocking faces surrounded him,

"Chicken."

"Chicken." Brian was sweating and knew that the others were enjoying his discomfort. Several of the boys' arms were grabbing at him. Jason was laughing and gesturing that they should pull down his trousers; Savannah was coming forward to oblige while some of the others attempted to lift Brian to stand on the back seat. They had almost succeeded, having managed to drag him on, so that his feet were actually on the fabric and he was being shoved into the upright position, but Brian's wretched state gave him sudden strength. He broke free and leapt down, pushing past the boys and knocking Savannah against the window, just as both teachers climbed back onto the coach.

"Brian Bottomley!" Mrs Harrison yelled, and several of Jason's gang started sniggering. Jason himself managed to stand there with a straight face, almost angelic, as the teachers came storming up the coach. Mr Field was first, and quickly realised the situation, but Mrs Harrison was already pushing up the aisle behind him. He was just about to speak when her shrill voice rang out. Mr Field remained silent but he raised his eyebrows high to show his irritation.

"Dear, dear Savannah. Are you alright? Sit down. Let me look at you."

"Thank you, Mrs Harrison. I'm just dealing with it. Please could you carry on getting the rest of the class off the coach."

"Mr Field I must protest. Savannah has been injured!" Mrs Harrison retorted angrily, forgetting all her training about being polite to other teachers in front of the pupils. "Mr Field, you're still quite new to this job, but surely you must see that I have to help Miss Smythely. Remember that her father is one of our Governors. I'm sure you would agree her health is of priority."

"The health of *all* the children is priority, Mrs

Harrison." Mr Field said quietly, but Mrs Harrison didn't move.

"Savannah dear, can you tell me what happened?" She asked gently, totally blanking Mr Field. Savannah was delighted, she dipped her head down as if embarrassed but then lifted her gaze, demurely, so that her eyes seemed larger than ever.

"Of course, Mrs Harrison." She began, hesitating a little, apparently nervous. Mr Field sighed, loudly, but Mrs Harrison and Savannah ignored him.

"Well, unfortunately Brian was going to do something very rude. He was going to..." She paused momentarily, seemingly unwilling to describe the very rude action. Really it was very well done, Mr Field had to admit, and Mrs Harrison was completely taken in. Savannah began again, speaking shyly and quietly in a very different voice to her usual one.

"We didn't think you would like it, Mrs Harrison, so we tried to stop him and instead he pushed me to one side. Isn't that right Jason?" She smiled at Jason coyly and he nodded very solemnly back. Brian bit his lip and looked furious, but said nothing. Mr Field looked at Savannah and pursed his lips, he knew she was lying, but he also knew that there was no point trying to get to the bottom of the matter now. It was likely that the rest of the boys would only back up Jason and Savannah. Getting Brian to tell the truth in front of them would not do the lad any good, and anyway the trip was already running late. Mr Field had to content himself with facial expressions only. He levelled a very stern scowl at the smooth countenance of Savannah but, as he told his wife that night, it was like water off a duck's back. Savannah shook herself carefully, so that her blonde hair fell neatly around her shoulders, and was clearly unperturbed, maybe even enjoying her triumph. He had more success with the warning look he gave Jason: the boy had the decency to avoid his eyes and appear a little ashamed. Meanwhile Mrs Harrison was glaring furiously at Brian.

"I will speak with you later, young man." She said sternly, and carefully helped Savannah down the aisle and off the coach. Mr Field shook his head at her departing back but said nothing; he had to shepherd the rest of the children off as quickly as possible. He did manage to give Brian a brief pat on the shoulder as he went past, in a friendly gesture which he hoped would cheer him, but Brian was chewing his bottom lip and barely noticed.

The class was subdued as they finally got down into the car park. Cassie and Laura stood silently together, well apart from everyone else. Looking about, Cassie felt slightly sick and dizzy, she presumed it was from the journey; she often got travel sick. Today the weather was so humid and the atmosphere so oppressive, perhaps that was the reason for this awful queasiness. At a single gesture from Mrs Harrison, the class joined up in pairs and formed a line that straggled towards the steps leading up to the dark building, which was their destination. Cassie and Laura were the last, for which Cassie was grateful, she tripped twice on the uneven path as the class wound along towards the entrance of the Brontë parsonage, but because they were at the back there was only Laura to notice, and so nobody teased her. Savannah was more interested in Jason at the moment, so she had dragged Poppy over to stand behind him, which gave Cassie some peace. At the door stood a narrow man, shrouded in dark clothing, who stared at the line of schoolchildren grimly. He consulted a list, before announcing pompously,

"You are expected, so of course your school is welcome,"

"Yeah, right." Matthew whispered to Jason, the man glared at Matthew but didn't pause.

"But you must remember to give due consideration to other visitors." The man added slowly and gravely. Most of the children nodded solemnly but one or two giggled, earning warning glances from Mr Field. The ponderous tones continued.

"The parsonage rooms can be small, and fire regulations insist that you go round in groups of six." He concluded, forcing a hasty consultation between the two teachers, who then addressed the class.

"Now children," began Mrs Harrison, "we're going to treat you like adults today, and let you go through this museum in your own groups. Mr Field and I are on hand, and there are lots of people dressing up in costume from the Brontë era; they'll be able to answer any questions you might have. At the end, there will be some craft activities from Charlotte Brontë's childhood, so make sure you all have a go. And, it goes without saying, don't anyone leave the museum!" Mrs Harrison looked at Mr Field for confirmation and he nodded, so she smiled at the class and stepped towards the door with the first group of six. The rest of the children swiftly assembled themselves with their friends. Savannah enjoyed deciding which of the many fluttering girls about her she would permit to be in her group, a task which involved disappointing several of her classmates. Afterwards she affected sorrow, but was unable to resist making a remark to her select group, loud enough to be overheard by the remainder, the four girls rejected by Savannah, and Cassie and Laura. This last group numbered the requisite half dozen, so Mr Field had nodded his satisfaction as he passed, counting. When she was sure Mr Field had gone out of earshot, Savannah said unkindly: "The dregs of society, Cassie's clumsy crew." The chosen girls giggled, the unfortunate ones tried to distance themselves from Cassie and Laura, just as Mr Field came along to usher them back together; their agitated expressions provoked more unkind laughter from Savannah's group.

"Now you six will be going in last so you'll have to be extra careful." He told Cassie's group, and then went off to start the second group on their tour. When they had entered, Savannah brought her group nearer to Cassie.

"You *will* have to extra careful, Cassie, I've heard the Parsonage is haunted."

"Haunted?" Poppy asked, clutching Savannah's arm anxiously. Savannah shook it off irritably.

"Yes, but you don't have to worry, Poppy. They won't be after *you*." She paused, and looked at Cassie slyly. "They only go after people who have family on the other side." As Cassie winced with the cruelty of Savannah's remark, Laura shot Savannah an angry look. Savannah grinned with delight.

"Ha, the mouse is angry with the cat, how quaint. Perhaps you should be in my group after all?" She extended a hand towards Laura, and the girls she had chosen looked at each other worriedly, but Laura put a protective hand on Cassie's arm instead. Savannah's eyes flashed angrily, and she was about to say something else, when Mrs Harrison came out of the Parsonage and stepped towards her.

"Come along, Savannah, dear, I'd like your group to come in now. I want to take a photograph of the dining room and I thought you might like to be in it?" Savannah threw back a satisfied sneer as she followed Mrs Harrison through the Parsonage doors.

There were only two sets of children left outside now. Brian had initially been surprised to find himself surrounded by Jason's cronies and was feeling flattered, until he caught a glance between Jason and Matthew which made his insides lurch. Now that they were outside on their own, temporarily unsupervised, he swallowed nervously, anticipating trouble.

"Tell Brian about the ghost, Mattie." Jason began , leering at Brian nastily.

"Mrs Harrison never said anything about a ghost, Jase." Matthew interrupted quickly.

"Mrs Harrison doesn't know, clever clogs." Jason answered irritably, he was watching beads of sweat form on Brian's forehead.

"Only Savannah knows, but even *she* doesn't know exactly who it is though." He paused for dramatic effect; Jason had been to drama lessons. "The ghost of a young boy who's all on his own and very, very lonely, he is. The poor thing wants someone to play with, another boy, and get this, *he doesn't care how boring he is!*" He looked at Brian meaningfully, then turned to Matthew.

"Don't you remember, I told you all about him?" Matthew soon caught on and played along.

"Of course I remember Jay, but I thought it was our secret."

"Well of course it is, Mattie," replied Jason sweetly, "How foolish of me to let slip. Sorry, Brian, old pal, forget I mentioned it."

"Hadn't we better go inside Jay," Tim put in, right on cue, "after all, we don't want to miss what we came for."

"How right you are, Timothy, of course we must. After you, Brian." Jason gestured, smiling blandly, his eyes searching Brian's face for signs of fear. Brian simpered nervously as Jason gestured for him to go in front, then Jason and Matthew walked swiftly up behind Brian, nudging him at the top step and forcing him to stumble into the Parsonage. Brian accidentally pushed against the curator in his haste, and earned himself a severe glare, and a muttered complaint, in the process. Jason and his friends followed carefully after Brian, their smooth, innocent faces looking up and smiling as they passed. They each gave a polite hello to the man in the doorway, and received a friendly greeting in return.

Chapter 6

When Jason's gang had gone in, Cassie and Laura's group were the only ones left. The door attendant had told the children to wait five minutes, to allow the others to go through the first rooms; Cassie was relieved, she didn't want to go in straightaway, she was still upset about Savannah's remark about ghosts. It wasn't that she was scared, though, Lizzie had stopped that for her a long time ago, when Cassie had still been fairly young. Cassie remembered she and Lizzie had been watching something scary on television. Cassie had been frightened, but instead of laughing at her like some older sisters might have done, Lizzie had turned the television off straight away, even missing the end of the programme, just so that she could sit down next to Cassie, and explain. Lizzie said that she did not think there were such things as ghosts. "So many people have never seen one. It's not very likely, is it."

"No." Cassie had agreed, relieved.

"But," Lizzie had added, smiling, "What about ideas?"

"Ideas?" Cassie was confused,

"You have ideas, don't you?" Cassie nodded, wondering where the questions were going.

"We can't see ideas, but they still exist, because we know everyone has them, well most people anyway!" Lizzie said, laughing. Cassie had laughed along too, then something else occurred to her.

"So ghosts might be real, after all?"

"Maybe so," Lizzie had said, patting her sister's arm reassuringly, "but even if they do exist, I'm certain they're not nasty or dangerous, only people who'd got lost on the way to Heaven." Lizzie had reminded Cassie of that time that she, Lizzie, had got lost on her first day at her new school, and had wandered round it looking for her friends, wandering round corridors and poking her head in-and-out of classroom doors, like a hamster goes round one of those complicated slot-together hamster houses. Cassie had laughed of course, as Lizzie had intended she should, and somehow the whole ghost business had never seemed so bad after that.

Until now. Savannah's remark had made Cassie distinctly uncomfortable. Cassie had never thought of her sister being a ghost, she certainly didn't like to think of her wandering, round and round, lonely and lost. She wanted to say something to Laura, but she had no idea what, and Laura was equally unsure. She didn't know what Savannah meant exactly, but she guessed it was something unkind. She didn't want to ask, in case talking about it might make Cassie even more miserable, so they both kept quiet, and stood staring at the front of the Brontë Parsonage as if it was the most interesting thing in the world.

At first glance the building seemed imposing, but after a while Cassie began to wonder if its apparent reserve was merely a front, and that really it was just a friendly family home. After all, Mrs Harrison had said that the children had lived and played here for much of their lives. They must have had some fun. It was a nice thought. Cassie's mind had started to drift again. She was half aware of the rhythmic rise and fall of voices nearby; the other four girls in their group were gossiping some short distance away, when, suddenly, there was a bursting effusion of excited conversation as three girls rushed out of the Parsonage entrance and glided effortlessly down the steps from the house. The girls were all dressed in old-fashioned costume, and Cassie watched them, utterly fascinated, as they came towards her and then passed by. She admired their ease of movements, if she wore a long skirt like that she would be sure to trip over it unless she went very slowly and carefully, but they all moved quickly, confidently oblivious to the constraints of the heavy, trailing material. They must have to dress up like that quite often for the museum, they've got quite used to it, Cassie thought, assuming that they were part of the Parsonage staff. She was impressed with the intensity of their role play; the three young women were all deeply immersed in their discussion, so much so that they didn't appear even to notice her, or Laura. She caught a wisp of their words, they were talking about the inhabitants of a country she had never even heard of. She must have got the name wrong, it was very strange: 'Angria'. As if someone was cross...

"Cassie!" Cassie jumped and looked round, surprised by how empty and autumnal the garden had become. Now there was only Laura in front of her. Laura had placed her feet on the bottom step of the three leading up to the door, so that she was as tall as Cassie; she was clearly ready to go in. Standing at the top was the figure of a man just coming out of the doorway, it was the curator, his lined face was peering with concern down onto them both.

"Are you alright, dear?" He asked Cassie, who stared back at him blankly.

"Is she alright, your friend?" he asked Laura, looking at Cassie rather doubtfully.

"Oh, she's fine, don't worry, just a daydreamer. Come on Cass, everyone else has gone in," Laura ordered, and Cassie looked round obediently, surprised to see that they were indeed alone in the garden, the other girls had disappeared.

"Where did they go?" Cassie asked, still dazed.

"The rest of our group?" Laura asked, "They went in, I just told you."

"No I meant those other three in the costumes." Cassie said bemusedly,

"What other three?" Laura asked Cassie,

"They came out of the door and went right past us." Cassie insisted, the curator looked at Laura and raised his eyebrows meaningfully.

"There's nobody been past here, love, you're getting confused. This is the entrance, not the exit." He looked at Laura and whispered.

"Are you sure she's alright? Why don't you let me fetch that nice lady teacher?"

Laura shook her head but didn't bother replying; she was too busy pulling Cassie up the steps and into the Parsonage.

★　★　★

Cassie's first impression on entering the hall was that it was icy cold and empty, bereft of all that was warm and alive. The chill of the air over the stone floor woke her up after the mugginess of the day outside, and she became instantly alert to her surroundings. They were supposed to turn right and go into that room first, but the rest of their group were already squashed in dutifully. Cassie and Laura stood in the doorway uncertainly; from the look of the row of immovable backs, held stiffly together, it seemed the others were determined to heed Savannah's words and distance themselves from Cassie and Laura. So intent were they on continuing this unspoken resolution, even though Savannah was nowhere in sight, that they had forced themselves to make a solid, unbreakable line in the narrow space between two rope barriers. However, as the girls saw Cassie and Laura attempting to enter the room they moved themselves forwards and pushed the rope barrier to the utmost. This set off the warning alarm, which brought the curator scurrying in quickly, gesturing importantly for Cassie and Laura to come out of the way. The girls stepped back into the corridor obligingly and exchanged a glance. They smiled, and automatically turned to cross the hallway and enter the room behind them instead. They were kept from going in properly by another barrier of rope. Cassie hadn't realised that the enclosed area was so small, when she turned to see if Laura was following her she tripped and clutched the rope to save herself as she fell forwards, wrapping it round one wrist and an ankle as she dropped. Instantly the shrill alarm sounded again. The curator came rushing over, followed by the rest of the girls from their group whom he had been in the middle of lecturing about the importance of the alarm system. When the girls saw Cassie tangled up in the rope, and struggling to get up, they burst out laughing. They found it even more amusing when the curator tried to help Cassie, while at the same time berating her for not being more careful. It was astonishing how knotted the rope had become,

Cassie thought, it must have wound round further when she had struggled to pull herself free. It was some time before the attendant succeeded in untangling her, and only when that had been completed did the loud, unkind laughter of the other four girls settle.

"We'll have to tell Savvy about this," one said loudly.

"Yes, she'll have to let us go round with her then."

"It would be cruelty to leave us with clumsy Cassie, she's bound to get us into more trouble if we stay with her." The girls rushed away in search of Savannah and the curator gruffly resumed his position at the front door, leaving Laura and Cassie standing dutifully in their allotted metre. Cassie's cheeks still flamed, she was scared to move in case she set the alarm off again, and Laura's timidity had returned with a vengeance. They stared forward, gazing without interest at the table, polished and posed, the paper and pen laid upon it, eternally waiting. The walls were equally uninspiring, decorated only with a few old pictures. Cassie gave a cursory glance at the one of a prim woman above the fireplace. Her eye was going to pass it and forget it, but she was drawn by the slightly wistful expression: there was a tiny, almost imperceptible, curve to the woman's lips making Cassie wonder if she'd found the whole portrait sitting thing a joke. She stared at the picture dreamily for a few minutes, until Laura tugged her arm gently.

"Shall we go?"

"Yeah. I was just wondering who that is?"

"Hang on, it'll be on this booklet Mrs Harrison gave us." Cassie looked at the booklet Laura was proudly carrying and sighed, she vaguely remembered being handed one as she got off the bus but already she had no idea where it was.

"Yes, it's here, that picture is Charlotte. Wasn't she the oldest of the Brontë children?" Laura asked without looking up; her eye was scanning the page quickly.

"Probably. She looks like she's struggling to keep a straight face."

"Are you sure?" Laura said doubtfully. "I thought everybody was very quiet and serious in those days." A loud guffaw broke out behind them.

"Quiet and serious? Those Brontë children? What are you thinking of?" And a delightful deep laugh deafened them again.

Laura and Cassie turned round in astonishment to find that an enormous person had crept into the room behind them, the speaker looked at their surprised faces with evident amusement. The middle aged woman was dressed in the most peculiar old clothing: an ancient apron, a cap on her head pulled down nearly over her ears, but with cosy, rosy cheeks and such a twinkle in her eyes, the two girls could not help but like her immediately.

"Are you their mother?"

"Gracious me, no!" There was more hearty laughter. "Now then misses, there's no need to make fun of a poor servant. You're just as bad as them childer o'mine, always playing tricks they is. Now I'm Tabby and can I ask what you are doin' in the middle of my dining room, if you please, when I have supper to get?" The woman again smiled broadly, rosy cheeks glowing, until Laura realised what was happening,

"Oh, of course, you're pretending to be the Brontë's servant, that's why you're wearing this costume."

"Well *costume's* a very fancy word for my working clothes I'm sure, and there's certainly no pretending involved! I never pretend to be anything that I'm not, but yon childer, those Brontë children, they are allus pretending something till it's no wonder that I can't stand any more. One time I had to go on to my nephew's house and send him up here. I daren't stop in the house any longer, the childer were all goin' mad. They set up a great crack of laughin' when they heard, it turned out that it had all been a big joke!"

"Are the children here at present?" asked Cassie politely, enjoying the role play. "I think one has just left the room," and she gestured towards a shawl casually draped across the back of the sofa, 'Tabby' peered over at it and then nodded.

"Oh yes," she replied, "that would be Em's. She's away at school now, but somehow I can't bring myself to move it, I get such a peculiar presentiment," She paused, and raised her eyebrows meaningfully at the two girls before turning to gaze at the shawl again. "It quite unnerves me so I always end up leaving it there." She sighed deeply before adding. "Just in case," and, curtseying slightly, she took her leave, exiting the room as quietly as she had entered it.

"I wonder what she meant," Cassie said, but Laura knew, she was flicking through her booklet again; when she found what she was looking for, she read it aloud for Cassie's benefit.

"'Tradition has it that this is the sofa on which Emily died.' Oh, that's awful, urgh, don't look at it Cass, let's go." Grabbing Cassie's hand Laura pulled her out of the room, but not before Cassie had had one last glance at the portrait over the fire, its subject staring longingly at the sofa. The room remained empty and expectant, the atmosphere itself in suspension, awaiting the return of the family.

Chapter 7

Across the hall was Mr Brontë's study. Once again, the girls stood carefully behind a roped barrier just inside the doorway, staring at the sparse furniture arranged in oddly staged symmetry. The room looked distinctly uncomfortable and Cassie and Laura curled their noses in distaste.

"I feel like a naughty schoolgirl just standing here. What must it have been like when he was alive?" Laura giggled and quickly looked behind, but there was no one there this time, ready with a quick tongue.

"Look at that magnifying glass!" Cassie said, reaching out her hand to point it out to Laura, but as she did so another, smaller hand slid past hers and picked the huge magnifying glass up from the desk in front of them, before pulling itself back quickly and disappearing out of the room amidst the shrill squealing of the alarm.

"BRANWELL!" yelled a thick voice from above, and the girls rushed out in time to see the backs of quick legs, encased in brown flannel trousers, disappearing round the corner of the stairs. The curator sitting by the door looked at them sternly, then scolded the pair.

"Just watch you don't set the alarm off again, it's a terrible nuisance. Your class teacher said you would be fine by yourselves but alarms are going off all over the place. We've got other people here besides you school-children you know!" and he tut-tutted at them and shook his head. The girls looked at each other, then Cassie plucked up courage and spoke,

"It wasn't us, sir, it was that boy pretending to be Branwell, he picked up the magnifying glass and took it upstairs."

The curator stared at her oddly before replying; when he did, it was with barely concealed anger.

"No boys have come past here. In this last five minutes all *I've* seen is girls coming in and alarms going off."

"But I saw..."

"Is there a problem?" Mrs Harrison appeared, hurriedly making her way down the staircase, she had evidently been listening. She was followed by a troop of children being led by Savannah, whose blonde head was just behind Mrs Harrison's shoulder, smiling angelically at the curator. The rest of Savannah's group and the four girls who had absconded from Cassie's were shadowing Savannah.

"Is something the matter?" Mrs Harrison asked again; the curator answered her sharply.

"Yes there is, I've had nothing but trouble from these girls. The alarms go off every time they go in a room and now they've just told me a pack of lies about a young boy running off with the magnifying glass. I've been here the whole time, and there's nobody has passed me, apart from them two."

"But there was a boy." Cassie insisted. The curator frowned once more and stood up, raising himself to his full height. Cassie looked at the man in dismay, he was taller than everyone else there and wore very dark clothes, his previous grim patience was now carved into anger, his brow as immovable as stone. The whole, solid stance of the man reminded her of something more, but she wasn't sure *what* exactly.

"A black pillar," a voice behind her said mischievously, and giggled. "Yes!" Cassie thought, that's exactly right! The man reminded her of a black pillar. Cassie turned round to say "Yes that's exactly it! How did you guess?" to Laura, but Laura looked glum and silent, and gave no indication of having said anything. She could see Savannah smirking and whispering to Poppy; it must have been *her* speaking, Cassie thought, rather surprised. Savannah was usually careful not to interfere in someone else's lecture, but perhaps she was getting complacent. Now Mrs Harrison will surely say something, Cassie thought, the voice had been so loud, and so Cassie was silent, expectant, waiting for Savannah to get a word of warning at the very least, but Mrs Harrison seemed to be pretending that she hadn't heard anything; she had already begun berating Cassie.

"Really Cassandra. I am very angry with you and your blatant rudeness in ignoring me. In the past I have indulgently referred to your behaviour as *daydreaming* but now you have begun to use these so-called daydreams as an excuse. Most people would just call what you do telling tales or, if they were really honest – lying!" She paused dramatically. Cassie was amazed that Savannah didn't get so much as a mention for butting in, but it was hardly a surprise. Mrs Harrison was about to conclude.

"You are a liar, Miss Edwards."

"That's not true!" The injustice of Mrs Harrison's lecturing made Cassie bold and, for once, she defended herself. "It's not lying or telling tales, Miss. The boy dressed up as Branwell picked up the magnifying class we both saw him..."

"Well that's simple," the curator interrupted sternly, "we don't have anyone dressed up as Branwell." That silenced Cassie, she glanced at Laura and could see that this was as much of a surprise to her as it was to Cassie. Meanwhile, as they tried to digest the meaning of this information, Mrs Harrison was apologising to the curator and Savannah was lapping up every word.

"I am so sorry. Yes she is a problem child, school and home I think, yes... Very disappointed, yes. Looking for the magnifying glass was her special mission, trying to be positive, you know... wanted to give her a chance to succeed *for a change*." She nodded, listening to the curator's reply, then shook her head sadly.

"I should have known something like this would happen, you just can't *trust* this type of child." The curator nodded and his eyes were still angry when they looked at Cassie. When Mrs Harrison had finished explaining she turned to Cassie.

"I am very disappointed in you, Miss Edwards. For one moment yesterday, I was pleased that you were actually showing some interest, but how typical of you to let me down. Hand over the magnifying glass to the curator please."

"But I haven't got it Miss, I didn't touch it." Cassie protested.

"Come in here, I'll prove it!" roared the attendant and pushed past Cassie to get into the Study. The girls squeezed back into the room, and so did Mrs Harrison and Savannah, so that they all packed into the roped off area. Cassie and Laura were amazed to see that the magnifying glass had not been moved at all, it was still in exactly the same place. For the first brief moment Cassie innocently thought that the curator and Mrs Harrison would be pleased by this, but she was totally wrong, they were angrier still. Savannah and her cronies watched with delight as Mrs Harrison's neck blotched into redness, and she began to splutter forth accusations with flecks of spittle still attached.

"For you to behave like this, Miss Edwards, you must think I'm a total idiot. You are deliberately and wilfully setting out to make me look stupid!" Mrs Harrison hissed. Cassie and Laura looked at each other.

"There *was* a boy," Cassie said, but her voice was weaker, "He picked up the magnifying glass, we both saw him."

"Lies, all lies!" The curator muttered, and Cassie fell silent. Mrs Harrison gave an apologetic glance at the curator and a fierce glare at Cassie, then with a grim, tight expression she started to usher the rest of the girls back out of the room, and gestured for them to go up the stairs. Savannah was out first, leading as usual, laughing and whispering. Cassie, at the very back, noticed Savannah's enjoyment and couldn't help but mutter something to Laura.

"Savannah must have had something to do with it." Unfortunately Mrs Harrison was within earshot and the remark was like a match to paper, her face flamed and instantly she swivelled round to face Cassie.

"Now, Miss Edwards, enough is enough. You have told enough lies to all of us, but involving Laura and now accusing Savannah is *despicable*. Savannah was upstairs the whole time; I was taking photographs of her group." She turned to the curator, her anger evident. The huge patches of red had spread, and risen up from her neck and on to her cheeks, flushing them almost purple under her make-up. Behind Mrs Harrison's back Savannah smirked and pointed at Cassie, gesturing with her friends and sniggering quietly. Savannah kept raising a finger to her cheeks and making a tiny sibilant sound, as if her finger had touched something very, very hot: "sss". Mrs Harrison seemed totally unaware of it, she was too busy talking about Cassie to the curator.

"Cassandra, I am sorry to say, is prone to deceit, but this little girl Laura, well," Mrs Harrison shook her head, "I can only say I am astonished. Miss Edwards is such a bad influence. If it weren't that I have already divided them into groups I might move her." She looked at Savannah wistfully, but Savannah had heard her and was busy whispering to her group. As soon as she felt Mrs Harrison's eyes upon her, she gave a single movement of her arm and all the girls, now in a group of ten, turned and walked up the stairs with one accord.

"We'll get on, Mrs Harrison, we don't want to miss out on any of our trip." Savannah called back in measured tones, emanating duty and responsibility. Mrs Harrison nodded, evidently pleased, she raised her hand to gesture gently in Savannah's direction.

"A model pupil." Mrs Harrison commented to the curator, who murmured agreement obligingly, and listened politely as she continued, "but then the family background is so different, her father is a governor..." She tailed off, suddenly remembering that Cassie was stood next to her, waiting. Mrs Harrison turned to admonish her, still convinced she was acting.

"Perhaps I will leave you as you are, so that you are not disrupting anyone else, Cassandra, but as you are clearly such a bad influence Miss Edwards, you must..." She paused, Cassie was looking back into the study with puzzlement. It was evident that she was not listening;

Miss Edwards was off in a world of her own again.

Cassie was indeed oblivious to Mrs Harison's words; she was standing and staring at the magnifying glass and thinking, 'I can't have been dreaming because Laura saw it too'.

It was too much for the patience of the teacher, she could endure no more. Mrs Harrison was absolutely furious. She forgot all of her professional training and shouted so loudly that the curate jumped, and several people popped their heads round the doors of the other rooms to see what was going on.

"ARE YOU LISTENING TO ME, MISS EDWARDS?" Cassie turned round quickly to face the teacher, her lip quivering, and even Laura looked tearful.

"Yes, Mrs Harrison." She mumbled sadly, watery tears welling up into her lower eyelid. She didn't want anyone to see, so she turned her gaze very slightly to look out of the open door and across the still damp lawn. Almost immediately her attention was caught by a bright glitter amongst the haze, which hung over a clutch of graves in the churchyard. The low light, sliding between the trees moved branches, and made it appear as if there was a small, illuminated figure bent over the graves, carefully sweeping moss from the inscriptions. 'I'm probably imagining that as well', she thought bitterly, and, hastily wiping her hand across her eyes, she raised her glance back to Mrs Harrison.

"I want you on your best behaviour in those other rooms now. You are a hardened girl, Miss Edwards; I don't know how to cure you of your terrible habits! Off you go." And without any further mention of the magnifying glass, Mrs Harrison dismissed them, and the girls were glad to go.

"'Hardened girl.'" The curator said, "It's odd that you should use that phrase."

"Oh?" Mrs Harrison was on the defensive. "Well, if you knew the problems I *have*."

"I'm not denying it," the curator said hastily. "I've seen what she's like, but it's odd that you should use the *exact* phrase that Charlotte Brontë uses for one of the teachers in Jane Eyre." Mrs Harrison was silent; she had just been rereading Jane Eyre, before she started teaching the class about the Brontës. She paused a moment while she thought, and suddenly she remembered the phrase. Then there was a cold sensation of guilt in the pit of her stomach: the teacher that the curator was referring to was portrayed as cruel in the extreme. Mrs Harrison was ashamed; she nodded briefly and went off quickly. The curator sat down again by the door and looked out across the churchyard, it was hazy, as it often was, and there was an odd looking sparkle reflecting on something right in the middle of a group of graves. He wasn't sure what it was that caused it, but he had seen it before. Sometimes, he put it down to the sunlight coming through the windows of the Church at a peculiar angle, and then bouncing off the trunks of trees; sometimes he blamed the damp for producing some sort of rainbow effect. He told himself again that it was only a trick of the light that seemed to make a ghostly outline, but still he shuddered involuntarily and swivelled himself round on his chair, so that he had his back to the sight and could only view the interior of the Parsonage. But today the inside of the house was not much better. The empty corridor seemed different from yesterday, more fuzzy, the outlines of the doorways were blurred and even the air itself was tremulous, almost palpable.

Atmospheric pressure, he decided, or possibly stress from all those alarms was affecting his eyesight; perhaps his glasses were the problem, did he need new ones maybe, or had these got fogged up without him realising? Irritably the curator took off his glasses and examined them. He looked at the clean, clear lenses and rubbed his eyes, then glanced up. For a moment he thought he saw a girl on the stairs, but when he replaced the glasses she was gone; he presumed it was another one of those kids messing about again. He sighed deeply; he hated school trips.

★ ★ ★

The booklet directed Cassie and Laura to the kitchen next, but, instead of the cosy nook Mrs Harrison had talked about in class, there was now a broad corridor, apologetically including a few of the Brontës' utensils, so the labels decreed. Today, despite the museum staff still using the room as a pathway, the girls found 'Tabby' in full swing at the table, busily baking bread for 'the family'. The warm, yeasty smell was mouth watering, and several of the boys had lingered in this room, chattering happily to the friendly Yorkshire woman in her working clothes, enthusiastically enjoying her drama.

"Aye and you'll be friends of the young master's, will ye? He does love to hang around on baking day! Aye, an' the children allus gather here of an evening, th' right enjoy ma stories. We all sit round the fire, they'll stay as late as I let them, they do not like going to bed them children!" Tabby shook her head in mock horror, causing laughter among the assembled children. She watched in satisfaction until they were quiet again, then continued her speech.

"Why I remember one night, last December it would be, aye, December of 1827. It was cold, bitterly cold. I wanted them to go to bed, they wanted to stay up and light a candle. The kitchen fire was blazing, and outside the piercing winds and snow storms of winter. Do you think you would like to be here then?" She paused to see if they could imagine the intense cold of the winter's night, as it would have been on the moors behind the bleak Parsonage. It was difficult in the muggy summer weather, most of the faces were blank, but one or two were there, she could tell by their pinched foreheads and dreamy, half-closed eyes. She recognised Cassie and smiled, and Cassie smiled back happily; she could nearly hear the wind howling round the walls and down the chimney, and feel the heat of the warm fire. She loved using her imagination, she wished every day at school could be like this, she would never need to resort to daydreaming again. Tabby picked up the dough and began kneading, telling the story in time to the push and pull motion of her hands. "In the end we compromised, they got a few extra minutes downstairs, I came off victorious in that no candles were produced. Young master Branwell's bored, he gets his little stubborn face on, all of ten years old but e's thinkin' hisself full grown and sighs a long, drawnout sigh, an' says 'I don't know what to do.' Emily and Anne started copying him and it was young miss Charlotte that said 'you're so glum Tabby', and then starts t'others off talking 'suppose we each had an island'. That was enough, they weren't bored anymore. They all mun have their own islands: Branwell picked the Isle of Man, Charlotte chose the Isle of Wight, Emily had Arran and Anne chose Guernsey. Then they must have ordinary folk on 'em, and they had these 'ere 'chief men' to be in charge. Charlotte would always have the Duke of Wellington and that's why there's a portrait of him in the dining room. After that they started telling stories of the Islanders. It wor right grand to hear as how they come oot with all these tales; I wor right capped wi' it." Most of the listeners stared, fascinated, but a couple of boys had noticed that a loaf of bread was by itself at one end of the table, within reach of one of their outstretched arms. The presence of Tabby had necessitated the deactivating of the alarm, so Jason had managed to successfully make contact with the loaf, and was just in the process of stealthily lifting it from the table, when Tabby spotted him.

"YOUNG SIR!" She bellowed, shocking Jason into dropping his prize back onto the wooden surface, making a sharp, crisp, crunch as it landed instead of the soft, nearly silent, slump of warm, freshly baked bread. Jason looked horrified, and even Tabby struggled to keep a straight face as she mock scolded him.

"Now see, young sir, I guess you've been at one of them schools that don't know how to feed children. Well, lad, I darn't begrudge you yon bait, but I mun have some for t'master, he allus has his tea at six with the family, you see. You come along at suppertime an' old Tabby'll see you right." She smiled warmly at Jason but he blushed then turned and fled from the room in embarrassment, conscious of his super cool image being singed. Matthew and Tim followed closely behind, pushing past Cassie and Laura as they went, then Brian sauntered out after them, chuckling to himself and smirking at Cassie and Laura as he passed them. He expected approving smiles, but although they had felt sorry for him on the bus, his smug satisfaction in Jason's rebuke was nauseating.

Chapter 8

The boys had gone into another room across the hall and soon the loud sounds of raucous laughter drew Laura and Cassie over, curious to see what was causing such hilarity.

"Listen to this," Brian was jeering. He was standing in one corner, attempting to read a board on which was written the Lord's Prayer in Victorian script. With his back to the rest of the room, he was being as irreverent as possible, in the hope of impressing Jason.

"Forgive them that trefpaffs againft uf," he sneered in a loud lisp. He was thoroughly enjoying the gratifying guffaws of Matthew and Tim, but he was especially pleased that Jason was also doubled up, his cheeks bright red with laughing. Brian thought that they were laughing at the way he was reading the old style writing, with its amusing substitution of the 'f' character for an 's', but he was wrong. Brian was completely unaware of the presence of a stern faced woman who had crept quietly into the room, just after he had begun speaking. She was suitably dressed in stiff, starched Victorian clothing; her back was straight, held in place by a tight corset under her jacket and collar; her hair was pinned harshly into submission, she was the picture of a strict unsmiling Victorian matron. The woman had placed herself right behind Brian and stood inches from his back, directing at it her fierce countenance and *literally* breathing down his neck. This was the sole cause of the two boys laughter. She allowed Brian a few more minutes, then, catching the eyes of Laura and Cassie and bestowing upon them a glimpse of a warm smile, she resumed her role and exclaimed loudly.

"What heathen child is this to blaspheme in the house of the Lord's Servant?" Brian jumped as if he had been shot and turned round rapidly, causing Jason and Matthew to become virtually insensible with repressed mirth. The Victorian woman gazed firmly at Brian, Cassie could tell from her expression that she understood perfectly what had been happening, there was sympathy in the face as it met Brian's miserable look, and annoyance as she glanced over to the corner in response to Jason and Matthew's continued snorts.

"Now, young man!" She began, Brian could hardly lift his face. Cassie and Laura gazed at him with pity, a few minutes ago they had seen him smirk at Jason's scolding, but now he looked so dejected they could not help but feel sorry for him. The woman saw it too, and the rest of her speech was given in more sympathetic tones.

"Bread and cheese for a week if you're staying here at the Parsonage, you and your friends must learn some manners. I'll be speaking to the Reverend Brontë about you, so run along!" Brian fled the room gratefully, this time it was Jason, Matthew and Tim who pushed past the girls, still chortling and sniggering. When the boys had gone, the woman turned to Laura and Cassie, who had remained silent.

"You two would have been alright in Victorian times, seen but not heard, don't you think?" she said kindly.

"That's not what my teacher thinks, Miss, she thinks I should be heard more often!" Cassie joked.

"That's cause you're always daydreaming, Cass,"

Laura put in, not meaning to be unkind, but Cassie's eyes filled up all the same. They were quickly spotted by the lady in costume, who bent down and patted her arm gently.

"A daydreamer, eh? You're in good company then." Both girls looked puzzled so the speaker continued. "Have you read the book Jane Eyre? Is that why your teacher brought you here today?" Cassie and Laura shook their heads silently, still bemused; their eyes focused with fascination on the woman as she spoke.

"Well, never mind. Why I asked is that in Jane Eyre there is a description of a school, a really awful school, not at all like they are now. One of the pupils there, Helen Burns, is a bit of a dreamer; she keeps getting into trouble for it. Charlotte Brontë wrote Jane Eyre when she was grown up, and she said that the character of Helen was actually based on her sister Maria, who was really, really clever with what Charlotte described as a wonderful mind, but – guess what – always daydreaming."

"Did she get into trouble with her teacher?" Cassie interrupted.

"Yes, unfortunately, and the one that Charlotte describes is a particularly unpleasant character. There was an outcry when the book came out. Some people said that what was written in Jane Eyre was so awful it couldn't possibly be realistic but other people, including some former pupils, recognised the school immediately. In fact, Charlotte sent a letter to her publishers to say that not only was the bit about the school true she had not written '*all*' for fear of it being too painful to read!" The woman paused, partly to let what she had told them sink in and partly because, out of the corner of her eye, she had seen the fleeting movement of a figure outside the room at the bottom of the stairs. The figure appeared strangely familiar. Cassie and Laura automatically turned round too, curious to see what the Victorian woman was looking at, but there was no one there. The two girls turned back to the woman expectantly and she turned to speak to them, expecting that they would want to ask her about the figure, and not sure what she might say. She was surprised that they didn't even mention it. For a brief moment the stern face of the Victorian Matron seemed uncertain then she smiled brightly at Cassie.

"From what your friend says about daydreaming, I think you sound just like Maria, Charlotte's big sister. Charlotte thought Maria was wonderful. That's what I mean when I say you're in good company, so don't you worry or get upset. Now I have to go into another room and talk to some other people, but I'll come and find you later and we'll talk some more, okay?" Cassie nodded, thinking that the woman was doing just what her mum always did, making up some story about some person who'd had just the very same thing happen to them, and how good it had been for them in the end.

"What happened to Maria then?" she asked eagerly, but the woman did not smile triumphantly, ready with the fairy tale ending, she merely glanced towards the door uneasily, patted Cassie's arm vaguely, and then straightened up, distancing herself from the girls.

"As I said dear, I must go round some other rooms now, I'm sure I'll see you again. Goodbye." Without waiting for a reply she left the room quickly, the sound of her hurried motion up the stairs belying the earlier casualness of the role play. The two girls remained in the silent room that had been the curate's study, politely admiring the remnants displayed: a bleak photograph of a chilly church, the prayer board and a piece of pew door. The objects were uninteresting to the girls, a glance for the sake of civility sufficed. Cassie was still thinking about the daydreamer the lady had spoken of.

"I suppose, because she was so brilliant, she got really famous and married someone rich, clever and handsome and they lived happily ever after."

"You're dreaming again, that only happens in films." Laura commented wryly. "Come on, we'll follow her. She can tell us herself then." The two girls left the room and headed for the stairs. As they trailed slowly up the worn steps, they discussed the identity of the stern, yet kindly, character.

"I wonder who she was meant to be?" mused Cassie, dreamily gazing down at the flattened stone, idly imagining the many illustrious and ordinary feet that had moulded these stairs.

"I bet it's their mum," Laura suggested from behind; she was trying to find out by reading her guidebook at the same time as walking.

"But she didn't look like a mum." Cassie said.

"How can you tell what a mum looks like? They're all different."

"That was Aunt Branwell." A voice said suddenly, making Cassie stop dead so that Laura collided straight into her. They were nearly at the top of the first flight of stairs, and were about to step onto the landing and turn to ascend the rest. The window directly in front of them flooded the staircase with light, the small alcove on the right had been hidden in shadow and neither had noticed the girl stood by the grandfather clock until she had spoken; somehow she had blended herself into the gap between the clock and the window. She was probably about their own age, but it was difficult to tell as she was dressed in such old-fashioned clothing. Her thin face was almost white and made paler by the proximity of the dark costume. Wisps of mousy brown hair were escaping from her lace cap. Her mouth was set straight, so that at first glance she appeared very serious and solemn to the two girls, but when they looked closer they saw that her eyes sparkled and twinkled, as if they lived quite apart from the grave features which surrounded them. No one said a word for a moment as all three gazed at each other, Laura peering round from behind Cassie, Cassie entranced by the girl's eyes and the girl herself squinting firstly at Cassie then at Laura. There was a further pause as each became aware that *someone* ought to say *something*, and then finally it was Cassie herself who overcame her shyness and spoke.

"Are you Charlotte, by any chance?" she asked gently. The girl looked at her, fleeting puzzlement swept across her face.

"I'm sorry," she answered, in a thick unfamiliar accent, "Do I know you?" Just then a shout came from upstairs.

"Talli!" The girl jumped, "Excuse me," came the strong brogue again, "I'm wanted."

"Talli? Is that your name?" Cassie asked, stung out of her normal reticence by her fascination with the character, but the girl only smiled, dipped her head ever so slightly in farewell and then ran up the second flight of stairs. Cassie and Laura remained, frozen in front of the clock. It had become colder and Cassie shivered slightly. The clock whirred and murmured incessantly before them, as if trying to tell them something. It reminded Cassie of the way a computer passed a message down a phone line. She'd picked up the extension sometimes when something was going through for dad, ages ago, when he'd still been working and had an office at home. Once, she'd listened for a moment to the burrs and beeps of the coded machine language, which was translated by her dad's computer into all sorts of useful information. She looked intently at the clock; the ornate hands; stately hour, leisurely minute, hurrying second. The figure at the top pleasant but mute. It all appeared perfectly normal and yet... Cassie got the feeling that if she turned away the clock would relax itself, the smiling woman at the top would rush off in a different direction and...

"Cassie! You're dreaming again, come on!" Laura exclaimed, and pushing Cassie forwards caused her to stumble and fall as they went up the next flight of stairs. Cassie clutched at the handrail and sank weakly down onto the top step, she was feeling dizzy and disorientated and the cool stone was soothingly solid. Laura looked at her, concerned.

"Don't you feel well?" Her nervousness was back again, her voice fluttery and anxious. "It's my fault, I shouldn't have pushed you. Gosh I'm so sorry. You look ever so white. I'll go and get Mrs Harrison, you wait here." Cassie did not reply but nodded and then dropped her head to her chest. Laura ran off shouting for the teacher, but the sound of her anxious calling was soon lost in the rooms beyond.

Chapter 9

Silence fell softly, muffling as fog. No voices were heard in the thick air. The atmosphere was so heavy; Cassie could feel the pressure across her shoulders as she lifted her head slowly to examine the scene through the window in front of her. Verdant moss half covered a tiled roof, bumped and curved at the edges, like the rolled out pastry she'd made for jam tarts at school. Good job they weren't green, she smiled, imagine what her dad would have said to that. The moss appeared to be glittering now. She concentrated hard on it, wondering if it was sunshine on drops of dew, or some other perfectly simple explanation, but as she watched, the image shimmered and changed. Before her eyes the bright iridescence faded and instead Cassie was looking at immense, inviting, stretches of distant hills, brown smudged with decadent flecks of rich purple. While she gazed, she became aware that she herself was being watched. In the gap between the window and the clock, the girl was standing again, staring at Cassie. Time was standing still, and they both knew it. In the quivering silent air they contemplated each other, then the girl seemed to make a decision. Lifting her shoulders and straightening her posture, she walked firmly towards Cassie. As she passed before the window she disappeared, as if the window was itself passing in front of her, but then she reappeared in the shadow at the other side, and stood on the steps below Cassie, insubstantial in her faded browns, but her eyes as brilliant as ever. Cassie was fascinated, she smiled at the girl. She felt no fear, instead she was strangely confident.

"You're her, aren't you?" she accused playfully. She was answered by a smile and the thick accent she now recognised as Irish.

"Now why would I be telling you anything? For all I know you're just a pixie." The girl's mischievous grin thrilled Cassie.

"*Me* a pixie, now that would be something. You're the one that keeps popping up all over, Charlotte Brontë!"

"Well, now, you're very formal, talking like that, it must be a Sunday!" Charlotte joked. Cassie smiled, her wave of dizziness gone, she felt exhilarated, as light as air.

"You're not at all like I imagined!" she remarked,

"Now, how would you be thinking of me, then?" Charlotte replied,

"Er, reading a book, sitting quietly in a corner somewhere."

"Now I reckon you've been talking to my friend Ellen! She'll tell you how quiet I am at school, to be sure, but home's different. You see Tabby, she'll be telling you. An' ask about *Talli*, never mind Miss Charlotte. Now you tell me your name, then we're properly introduced."

"My name is Cassandra Edwards, but you can call me Cassie."

"It's a pleasure to know you Cassie, now I see your folks are coming so I'll bid you good day." And with a hearty handshake the girl stepped back, as Mrs Harrison appeared from Branwell's studio with Laura nervously following behind.

"Cassandra, what has happened?" Mrs Harrison

enquired anxiously. She was still feeling guilty about calling Cassie a hardened girl, and she was determined to make amends; crouching down at the top of the landing. Mrs Harrison gently put her hand across Cassie's forehead.

"You're not particularly warm," she muttered, more to herself than anyone else. "How are you feeling now, dear?" Mrs Harrison murmured, peering into Cassie's eyes carefully, "Laura says you were dizzy and fell, she was quite concerned." Cassie beamed back.

"Oh, Mrs Harrison, Laura, it was lovely! I met that girl who dressed up as Charlotte Brontë."

"Cassandra, there isn't anyone dressed up as the children themselves," Mrs Harrison said curtly.

"Are you sure? I saw her, and Laura did too. She didn't definitely say it was her, actually she said, 'never mind Miss Charlotte', come to think of it." Cassie looked dubious for a moment, but then carried on enthusiastically, her head bent to look at the Grandfather clock where it seemed that Talli had appeared from. She pointed down the staircase to show Mrs Harrison, who turned automatically, to see nothing but a small dark shadowy space between the clock and the wall.

"But as I was just sitting here on the step she appeared on the stairs, they must have a hidden door in there, Miss, and we talked and she wasn't a bit like I imagined, much more fun and..." As Cassie spoke, Mrs Harrison's expression changed, her face lost its smooth gentleness and became taut, the skin between her eyes forced itself into thick ridges. When Cassie turned from gesturing to the Grandfather Clock, and talking excitedly to look into Mrs Harrison's face, instead of the shared enthusiasm she expected, she met the teacher's grim, stony expression. Immediately Cassie ceased her exuberant speech. There was a prolonged pause, then Mrs Harrison spoke, slowly and coldly.

"Miss Edwards, I have thirty-two children in this class to take care of today, thirty of which are now stood outside this museum, doing absolutely nothing, other than standing outside and waiting for you. I understood that some accident had befallen you and came rushing up here with Laura, who was terribly concerned, and then you have the insolence to regale me with yet more of your ridiculous daydreams."

"But Miss..." Cassie began.

"Don't interrupt me! This is utterly appalling, selfish behaviour and I will be speaking with your parents about it. Now get up, get outside and apologise to the rest of the class!" With that, Mrs Harrison drew herself up to her full height and left the girls. She marched rapidly across the landing and through Branwell's studio, her metal heels resounding as they hit the floor. Laura stretched out a hand to Cassie to help her up, which was taken gratefully. Cassie's eyes had filled with tears and she held her head down. Not a word was spoken, but as the girls left the old parsonage for the modern exhibition rooms, Cassie lifted her head and turned for one last look. At the top of the stairs, the girl, Talli, stood, brown clothes against dark doors effectively concealing her from a first glance, but as Cassie watched, the girl lifted her hand in a weak attempt at a wave, then abruptly dropped it, as her gaze shifted to Cassie's side. Cassie turned to find Laura looking at her oddly. Simultaneously they both turned back to look at the top of the steps. A group of tourists, loud of voice and dress, were now on the landing, exclaiming noisily as they entered the rooms which neither girl had managed to visit. Cassie opened her mouth to speak, but Laura tightened her grip on Cassie's arm and swept her in the direction Mrs Harrison had taken.

"Quickly, Cass, remember they're waiting." Cassie nodded, and the two girls quickly ran through to catch up with Mrs Harrison. The teacher refused to acknowledge their presence and strode purposefully to the exit in silence, passing the displayed remnants of the Brontë's life without pointing anything out to the girls or commenting in any way. They moved quickly through the shop, where a couple of the girls from their class still lingered over the sales racks, hiding behind the central display of goods when they saw Mrs Harrison coming, and then quickly and surreptitiously followed the teacher as she swept majestically outside to stand at the front of the class. Now Mrs Harrison stopped and turned, without noticing the other two stragglers at all, to gesture that Laura and Cassie should remain at the top of the steps, where they collided clumsily into each other like circus clowns. Savannah laughed loudly and most of the rest joined in; the class were bored of waiting and glad of some diversion. The line of children stretched out along the stony footpath, it was a short distance to the moors, Cassie could see them through a glittering haze. Mrs Harrison was talking to Laura.

"Now I know it's not like you, and it's not your fault you had to be paired with Cassie. Mr Field explained what happened this morning, so you go and join the line of children." Laura wanted to say something, she wanted to stick up for Cassie and say that she, too, had seen Charlotte Brontë, but years of keeping quiet had taken their toll. She remained by Cassie's side, biting her lip, thinking, and turned to Cassie to see what she wanted. One look of desperation would have given Laura the courage to speak, one word would be enough, even a single "Laura?" would have sufficed and Laura would have spoken, but Cassie's head was turned off in the direction of the distant moorland. She didn't even seem aware that Laura was beside her.

"Laura join the class please." Mrs Harrison said again.

"She can stand next to me, Miss," Savannah said helpfully. "I'll keep an eye on her."

"Yes." Mrs Harrison nodded, "That's kind of you to take care of her, thank you, dear."

"Oh, we'll take care of her, won't we Poppy *dear*?" Savannah grinned; she was hoping for full scale tears now that Cassie was going to be on her own. Laura looked at Cassie helplessly but Cassie was still absorbed in the view, her head turned away, oblivious, so Laura went meekly and obediently to join the class between Savannah and Poppy.

"Now, Miss Edwards, as you have held us up for so long, what have you to say?" Mrs Harrison addressed Cassie sharply; she sighed when she received no reply.

"She's not listening again, Miss." Poppy pointed out, rather obviously. The class watched, interested.

"Cassandra! Pay attention!" Mrs Harrison barked, and again louder still, "CASSANDRA, listen to me!" Heads popped out of the shop, withdrew back in again quickly, not wanting to be thought nosey, a couple with matching rucksacks walking down to the parsonage looked back and bent their heads together, muttering, and finally Cassie obligingly turned her head towards her teacher. She was clearly puzzled; Mrs Harrison must have been talking but what had she said?

"Dopey's in dreamland." Someone else called out but the voice went unchallenged by Mrs Harrison, who stared at Cassie with distaste.

"The whole class can see you, Cassandra Edwards, and I have explained how your daydreams have led to delay, yet again, so that we will not have time to finish the activities kindly provided by the Parsonage staff. Now, what have you to say?"

"I'm sorry," mumbled Cassie.

"What did she say?" Savannah asked, feeling brave, since her earlier remark had gone unnoticed.

"I don't know." Poppy said, playing along. Cassie heard them, and as her eyes flickered in their direction, for the first time she realised that Laura stood between them. Cassie was amazed: how had Laura got there? It was only a minute ago she was standing with me, she thought sadly. Tears pricked in Cassie's eyes, she stared hard at Savannah, but the triumph in Savannah's expression was too much to bear, and Cassie dropped her gaze to the floor.

"We can't hear you so say it louder!" The teacher ordered, clearly irritated. Sweat beaded on her brow, it was a hot day now that the earlier mist had gone. The waiting children shifted uncomfortably, they were eager to move, and, apart from Savannah's group, had little patience with the teacher's insistence on a repeated apology.

"Well?" Cassie looked up, she couldn't ignore Mrs Harrison for much longer, her eyes were brimful of water, automatically she raised a hand and brushed away a tear. Savannah was delighted and nudged Poppy excitedly, Laura looked miserable; Cassie twisted her head quickly to mop up the rest of the tears without Savannah seeing and found herself looking in the direction of the hills again. Suddenly she noticed something that she hadn't seen before: further up the path from the class, right along the footpath where the moors edged towards the village, stood a figure. She blinked, her brimming eyes and shimmery vision made her imagine there was someone vaguely familiar standing there. Cassie smeared away her tears so that her eyes were clear, this time she was certain the person was definitely there, and she knew who it was: Talli. Even at this distance Cassie could see a faint wisp of a mouth but those eyes; what light they had within them, it was as if the sun itself was shining from within. Cassie smiled, she was sure the figure smiled back.

"Miss Edwards!" Mrs Harrison shouted. "For the final time."

Cassie turned back swiftly, her head held high, that brilliant light in Talli's eyes gave her courage and she replied loudly and very clearly, with just a hint of arrogance.

"I apologise to the class for keeping them waiting." She looked directly at Mrs Harrison and met her gaze firmly. Mrs Harrison was disconcerted, Cassie looked quite unlike herself; she was sure Cassandra was staring right at her and she was almost tempted to accuse her of being rude, but there was such a dazzling brightness about her, Cassie must be standing right in front of the sun, how inconsiderate. In the end it was the teacher who dropped her eyes first, she looked down towards the village and motioned the children along without looking at Cassie.

"Well, that's better, we can all go now." Mrs Harrison and the front of the line snaked out of sight, Cassie turned back to see the outline of the figure of the girl. She was still standing on the path which led to the moors, which now appeared much nearer, some trick of the light Cassie presumed, so that it seemed as though the brown earth itself was reaching tentatively towards Talli, with feathery ferns clutching like fingers at her skirts...

"Dreaming again Cassie?" Savannah called loudly and Cassie realised that she had again been transfixed. Savannah was hanging back to taunt Cassie, and stood grinning broadly with Laura by her side. Laura was clearly unhappy, she stood with one of Savannah's manicured hands laid possessively on her arm, but Laura kept shifting her feet anxiously, trying to step away, and although she said nothing, she was nervously biting her lip. Savannah put her arm around Laura's shoulders, so that if Mrs Harrison looked round, she would not observe Laura's anxious behaviour. If Mrs Harrison turned to inspect them now, it would appear that Savannah was being kind and protective towards Laura, entirely fulfilling her promise. Cassie glanced back to see if Talli was still there, hoping that the sight of her would make dealing with Savannah easier, but the moors had receded again and the place between the flinty footpath and the intricate workings of the dry stone wall was empty, there was no sign of the figure of Charlotte Brontë, or whoever it had been.

Cassie was disappointed but not surprised, she began her walk to catch up with the rest of the class, with a heavy tread. Her head bent downwards, and she tripped twice over her own feet, until finally she stumbled on an unseen stone and fell to the floor just in front of the three girls. Savannah was brimming with delight, she had been hanging back waiting for just such an opportunity, and she was laughing even before Cassie hit the ground, a hard raucous laugh. Laura bent towards Cassie to pick her up but Savannah yanked her back swiftly, linking her arm tightly around Laura's quickly and indicating to Poppy that she should do the same.

"Now, now, Laura, Mrs Harrison is very concerned that you don't mix with the wrong sort, and Cassie is most definitely *the wrong sort*. Poppy and I will show you what true friends are really like!" And so saying she swivelled rapidly on her heels, turning her back on Cassie, and to her horror walked right into Mr Field, who had just come out of the Parsonage shop after checking that the last few pupils were gone.

" Well fancy bumping into you here, Miss Smythely." He began sarcastically, his expression clearly showing his understanding of the situation. Savannah's consternation was evident and she quickly dropped Laura's arm. Laura immediately bent to help Cassie, who was getting herself up from the ground. Mr Field also turned to check her over quickly, and brush the dust from her sleeves, before turning back to Savannah.

"Now that you are at the back of the class, and not the front, am I to presume that Mrs Harrison has seen the error of her ways and left you behind?" With the mention of her ally Savannah regained a little of her composure.

"Not at all, sir," She said, as imperiously as she could manage. "Mrs Harrison has asked us to look after Laura." Mr Field raised one eyebrow.

"Indeed? Well I'm sure Cassie and I can manage that adequately enough. Perhaps you should get back to your other duties?"

"Other duties, Mr Field?"

"Being photogenic for Mrs Harrison. I believe you have the role of *acting* the model pupil down to a fine art." He spoke without humour so that Savannah could not mistake his meaning.

"Come on, Poppy," She said, "Mrs Harrison will only be wondering where I am."

"Yes, don't keep your audience waiting!" Mr Field called after them, then he turned back to Cassie and Laura, playfully wagging a finger.

"Now you two shouldn't be lagging behind, so I am going to have to keep my eye on you." And saying that, he solemnly reached his right hand up to his eye and pretended to fumble for a moment, as if removing it. Cassie and Laura looked at each other and started giggling, Mr Field grinned and then shepherded his little group rapidly in the direction of the rest of the class.

Chapter 10

The remaining time flew by and afterwards Cassie found it impossible to remember where they had been after the Parsonage. In the kitchen that night her mum teased her, enjoying seeing her daughter so animated.

"So they had people dressed up and you met the one dressed as Charlotte Brontë, what was she like – did she sit in a corner with her nose in a book all day?"

"No I told you, mum, I'm pretty sure she was playing hide and seek, she came out from behind a clock."

"She came out from behind a clock and said, 'Hi I'm Charlotte Brontë'?" Lorna looked perplexed.

"No, mum. Her real name is Talli, and she didn't come out from behind the clock, she sort of materialised out of the air, but it was right *next* to the clock."

"How on earth did they manage that? They must have some really good special effects." Lorna muttered, her head bent over the potatoes she was peeling.

"...and later she was up the track when we came outside."

"The same girl, or was it another one wearing the costume?"

"The same girl."

"They must have a back way out then, Cassie. Or did you imagine her?" Lorna asked teasingly.

"No, mum," Cassie's eyes filled with tears. Lorna looked up from peeling and saw them, and a knot of fear twisted in her stomach. She hated Cassie being miserable.

"So, let me ask a different question. Where did you have your packed lunch?"

"Packed lunch?" Cassie said blankly.

"Yes, your sandwiches and crisps, I presume you ate them somewhere. Now, what is there in Howarth, it's a long time since I've been? Where would the teachers take you for your packed lunch, I know – did you have a picnic down by the river?"

"Is there a river, Mum? I didn't see. We did go down a very steep street, if that's any help to you. I remember because Mr Field kept pretending to fall down it. Then there were loads of funny looking shops. Mr Field kept saying daft things about them. I'm not sure where we actually had our packed lunches in the end, because while we were eating them Mr Field was telling us a story, so I was busy listening to that instead." Cassie's expression was so serious, and her face so pained by the effort to recall where they had eaten their sandwiches, that Cassie's mum laughed out loud, prompting her dad to wheel himself through from the living room to enquire what the joke was.

"Oh, you should have seen Cassie's face when I asked her where she'd had her lunch, what a picture!" Mike stared at them both oddly, then frowned, and started to wheel himself back through again. The abrupt departure immediately dampened their spirits, prompting his wife to call encouragingly after him,

"Guess you had to be there!" but he only paused without turning round, his shoulders tensed; Cassie thought he might speak but he moved off again without comment, his silence polluting the relaxed atmosphere. It was at these times that Cassie most missed her elder sister Lizzie. Lizzie had always brought a smile to their dad's face. On an evening, when he had come home from work and had his tea, he and Lizzie automatically retreated into the lounge and they would read the paper together. Cassie would have joined them if she had been able to read as well as Lizzie. Lizzie was brilliant at reading, she never got confused by the long words and the letters didn't move about like they did when Cassie tried to read. Cassie had never been jealous of her because Lizzie had always shared her gift. Reading came so easily to her that she had been surprised to find her younger sister struggling with it, so had spent hours looking at books, especially the Jacqueline Wilson ones, with Cassie, then more time showing her all her favourite magazines and once making Cassie her very own magazine that she could read herself. '*The Lizzie's Laughter magazine*' Lizzie had called it. Suddenly Cassie recognised that it was very similar in design to *Branwell's Blackwood's magazine* and realised that Lizzie must have done the same projects at school. She'd probably made her magazine at the same time as she was studying the Brontës. Cassie sighed: it would have been great to talk about the visit to the Parsonage with Lizzie, she would have been excited to hear about that girl pretending to be Charlotte Brontë, even if it was a daydream she wouldn't have cared. Lizzie never minded Cassie's daydreams, she said they often gave her great ideas for games and stories. Cassie's eyes filled with tears as visions of her sister flooded her mind. She slid silently down from the table and slunk up to her bedroom; her mum watched her go and, not wanting to ask the reason why, said nothing.

★   ★   ★

Next day at school, Mrs Harrison told them all that as *certain people* had held up the whole class, causing them to miss out on the Victorian activities she had arranged at the museum, the museum staff had kindly sent some quill pens and ink for the children to try out at school. The teacher glared at Cassie, causing all the children to look round and making Cassie's cheeks blaze hot and red. There was silence, but Cassie defiantly held her head high and looked straight forward, suspecting that Mrs Harrison was enjoying the situation rather too much.

After her ominous pause Mrs Harrison continued, "As well as the quill pens the museum also sent some quilling tools. I did point out to some of you the beautiful quilled box that Charlotte herself made."

"That old brown rubbishy thing miss!" shouted Brian rudely, looking about for approval, "It was manky!"

"Brian Bottomley!" shouted the teacher, "That box will still be admired long after you have quit this mortal sphere! Now if you think you can do better, you will have the chance this afternoon, but first, the literacy hour!" Now all heads were turned to Brian whose cheeks also flushed while the teacher stared at him, but as soon as her back was turned he looked across to Jason for approval. Jason was sitting at the far side of the class, near the door leading into the corridor, his head attentively facing forward, behaving exactly as a model pupil should. Jason encouraged the rest of the gang to think he sat like this in order to make fun of the recognised class swots, but actually, there were times, like when Mrs Harrison did the stuff about the Brontës, that he really did want to listen, and this was one of them. Brian was disappointed, but at least Matthew, sitting at the desk just behind Jason, was ready to look encouragingly across. He gave an impish grin while Mrs Harrison's back was turned, and quickly passed Brian a rolled up piece of paper to flick at the teacher. Brian was unsure at first but Matthew gestured so obviously that the rest of the class were beginning to look over. Fearful of being called chicken again, Brian flung the piece of paper with one flailing hand at the back of Mrs Harrison's curled hair, hoping that the paper would catch in the perm and therefore fall off unnoticed. Unfortunately for him, Mrs Harrison turned round just at that moment and the paper caught her right between the eyes, causing her whole countenance to explode into a purple rage. For one moment the teacher was so angry that she was speechless. The blush on Brian's cheeks faded to a bleached white; even he realised that he had gone too far this time. Most of the class were turned in his direction, watching carefully, only Cassie continued staring out of the window and Jason still faced forward, seemingly uninterested in the proceedings.

"What did you think you were doing, Bottomley?" Mrs Harrison asked finally, keeping her voice level although it grated on the nerves of everyone listening.

"Er, practising my quilling, Miss." Brian replied; realising that he was already in so much trouble had made him flippant. Still Jason did not turn round but several of the gang tittered and Matthew gave a small thumbs up sign which gave Brian the encouragement he needed.

"Brian Bottomley," Mrs Harrison shouted furiously, so that every eye was upon her and even Cassie turned quickly round and stopped daydreaming. Mrs Harrison paused, looking at the boy and seeing his pathetic pride in his peers approval, something in her hard exterior crumbled and when she started again she spoke wearily, as if even the words were worn. "Brian Bottomley, I refuse to cast pearls before swine. Children like you are two a penny. I've seen hundreds of you, every one the same." Here she paused, and looked round the class with a sigh. Cassie sat motionless, waiting for Mrs Harrison's gaze to fall on her, when it did Mrs Harrison began speaking again.

"You're not even worth the breath I am using to say this." She seemed to be saying it right at Cassie, even the others noticed, quite a few turned round and stared; Cassie's stomach squirmed downwards and tears pricked at her eyes. Mrs Harrison turned back to Brian. "Yet I am expected to educate you and teach you right from wrong!" She sighed again, looking at no one in particular. "It's no use, Mr Bottomley, I'm going to have to consult a higher authority: I'll take you along to the Head's office." With that she took Brian out of the classroom by grasping his jumper firmly but being careful not to touch his arm. Brian allowed himself to be led meekly, risking only one look back at Jason who was thoughtful and didn't even notice Brian's departure. Brian's disappointment was evident; he had no idea whether he had scored a victory or not. Cassie was relieved that Mrs Harrison's anger had been diverted but the whole experience left a bitter taste in her mouth. She was too indignant to daydream even: she was shocked by the teachers bitter outburst and one thought kept running through her mind: if Mrs Harrison hates teaching that much and we hate being here, then what is the point? One or two others were also pensive, especially Jason, he looked towards the window, chewing his lip slowly, and as he gazed out his eyes met Cassie's

which were turned towards the classroom door. Cassie was embarrassed and was about to put her head down when something in Jason's expression made her hesitate: his deep brown eyes were looking at her, not through her like they usually did, and he was deep in thought. She returned his gaze tentatively, then gave a gentle smile. Jason's eyebrows furrowed momentarily in confusion as he realised that Cassie was looking at him and smiling, but then his face changed and he reciprocated with one of his trademark grins. Cassie was thinking how different he appeared today, how much nicer he seemed, and Jason was thinking the same about Cassie. For a moment they stared at each other, oblivious to the rest of the class, so that when Savannah turned round to wave at Jason, neither Jason nor Cassie noticed. As Savannah realised who it was that Jason was looking at her eyes narrowed and the blood went out of her face. At that moment Mrs Harrison crashed back into the classroom and all the pupils sprang to attention and faced forward, their faces equally bland. Only a close observer would have noticed the hint of a smile at the edge of Cassie's mouth and the deliberate, pensive chewing of Savannah's bottom lip.

★　★　★

At dinner that night the family sat at the long table that had once seemed just right but now, without Lizzie, was enormous. They each felt her absence far more because of the continued mealtime tradition, but no one could bring themselves to utter their thoughts, so there they all remained, every evening, in silent contemplation. Tonight, however, Cassie's mum was determined to be cheerful.

"Cassie, darling I have a surprise for you!" Cassie had been staring down at her plate and all the while she was going over what Mrs Harrison had said, 'not even worth the breath I am using to speak this'. It was really getting to her, she wanted to say something to her parents, something about Mrs Harrison, but she didn't know how.

"What is it?" she replied to her mum, without looking up. She spoke in such a surly tone that her dad was prompted out of his nightly reverie.

"Cassandra! At least be civil to your mother, politeness doesn't cost anything."

"Sorry, Mum," Cassie muttered, customary tears welling up instantly, irritating her father even more.

"It doesn't matter, Mike," Cassie's mother soothed, "She's probably tired."

"She still shouldn't talk to you like that. It's ridiculous. I was never allowed to talk to my parents like that, Lizzie would never have..." He stopped, six eyes were filled with tears now and they all gulped them back. Nobody spoke.

Cassie had a desperate urge to say something, anything, that would make it all right again, but she didn't know where to start. She kept silent, pushing forkfuls of food between her lips and rolling them round her mouth as if they were made of stone. It was nearly impossible to swallow, her throat was so constricted with the effort of holding everything in. Finally her mother spoke, wearily and without enthusiasm.

"Because you seemed so erm, cheerful, yesterday." She paused – was she saying that Cassie was not usually happy, could she admit to herself that her daughter was clearly having problems? No, Lorna could not. Hastily she qualified her words.

"Of course I'm not saying that you're not normally cheerful... it's just that yesterday after you'd been on the trip to the Brontë Parsonage you were, well er, *particularly lively*, especially when you were chattering on about meeting that girl, Cass." She smiled nervously, "So, I went to the library to see if there was somewhere similar we could take you, more local. Apparently there's a place called Oakwell Hall not too far away. The Library Assistant said Charlotte Brontë used to visit there when it was a school. One of her books has a description of the Hall in it, "Shirley." I think the man said it was. Anyway, I checked on the map and it doesn't look *too* hilly, so your dad can come too." Lorna looked guiltily across at Mike, wishing that the last sentence hadn't slipped out. Mike turned to look out of the window, unable to meet her gaze. His chin set firm, he stared in fierce concentration at the strange golden twilight, battling with his emotions. The evening air trembled, shimmering with possibilities, the wonderful light soothed his nerves, seductive in its promises. It was his favourite time of day, and his wife and daughter knew it and were silent. All too quickly the gilded minute passed, but the warmth remained in Mike's face. He turned back to his family and stretched his arms across the table to take a hand from each, and enfold it gently in his own.

"It sounds great," he said. "When are we going?"

Chapter 11

Saturday dawned overcast but by ten o'clock the clouds had gone, swept briskly away by an impatient breeze. The whirling wind made Cassie restless and eager to be off. She looked out of her bedroom window at the row of similar houses opposite, all with the identical symmetrical faces and bland bricks. The sight made her rush downstairs to hurry their departure. As she dashed into the dining room she knocked off a picnic box placed on the edge of the pine table. It crashed to the floor loudly, bringing her mum rapidly out of the kitchen, her hands full of dirty breakfast dishes. Seeing her daughter amongst all the fallen items, Lorna gave a heartfelt sigh which made Cassie's heart sink.

"Sorry mum, Shall I take those?" she offered nervously. "Let me help you." Lorna shook her head wearily and went into the kitchen to put the dishes in the sink. Having dispensed with one chore, she came back into the dining room, and bent down to begin picking up the carefully prepared sandwiches, sausage rolls cooked that morning, and the Scotch eggs she'd eagerly bought at the butchers yesterday, after her visit to the library. Lorna had been so excited and pleased to be planning a trip and a picnic; it had felt like a great achievement, and now it had all come to this.

Cassie was trying to help her mum, but her nervousness made her fingers fumble and she seemed to be dropping more things than she picked up. It was extremely irritating the way things always unwrapped themselves as soon they got into Cassie's hands. There was a loud sniff from behind and Cassie realised that her mother was watching her. She turned and smiled apprehensively, but Lorna suddenly sank to the floor, dropping the sausage rolls and scotch eggs she had been cradling, and buried her face in her hands. Cassie watched her for a moment, wondering what to say. Loud sobs were coming from under her mother's arms. Cassie stood in silence, her hands anxiously moulding the packet of sandwiches she clutched. Tension was making her palms sweaty, which made the clingfilm unravel, so bits of grated cheese were squeezing out of the side and dropping onto the floor. Cassie felt useless, utterly useless; actually she felt *worse* than useless because she made more mess by trying to help. That made her the opposite of useless which she thought must be useful but that couldn't be right. In fact she was so weird and different there wasn't even a word for her. She felt sick.

She didn't know how long she stood there, staring at the hunched, crying figure of her mother. It felt like hours, but it couldn't have been more than minutes. The trance was broken by the sound of the post being dropped through the letterbox. For a moment, she thought it was dad coming back from the shop. He'd wheeled himself round, as he liked to do every morning, to get the paper. He could have had it delivered, Lorna had suggested it once, but the look on Mike's face had silenced her. Mike liked going to the shop because he did not get any special attention when he was in there. Neither the shopkeeper himself, nor his assistant, ever made a fuss of Mike and they had never "helpfully" suggested that Mike have his papers delivered. On more than one occasion, Mike had been in the shop when the paperboy collected his bag. Mike had recognised him as a neighbour living only two doors away, still the shopkeeper said nothing; Mike was extremely grateful. It took Mike quite a while to wheel himself round, the pavements weren't that brilliant, but he liked to be out, and feel the muscles of his arms gripping and pushing; he could get quite fast sometimes, but today he'd been gone some time. That meant that Cassie didn't have long to get things tidied up before he got back, and she desperately wanted to get things cleared up before he saw the mess *in case...* in case what? She wasn't sure, and she didn't want to try and imagine. She wasn't sure of either of her parents anymore. Her mother, the one person who had carried the family through the last months, by her determination to be okay, her persistence in trying to be cheerful, the pretence that they were all fine, was now sunk into a shuddering heap on the floor. Her dad had become an unknown quantity. Before, when Lizzie was about, Mum and Dad had been like two sides of an old stone bridge, moulded together, without any sign of a join in the middle. Lizzie and Cassie had relied on the bridge to get them across the water safely, they had grown up with its solid, worn dependability utterly taken for granted, and they had never stopped to think about the bridge other than to lean on it, and lazily admire the view of the world about them. Since the accident the bridge had become unstable, cement was coming out of the tiny gaps between the bricks, gaps that she had never even noticed before, and even as she tried to cross on it, she knocked more bricks out with her clumsiness. All she could do was scrabble on to the crumbling structure, and try to get a grasp, before she fell into the swirling rapids below. She was floundering, she knew. She had to do something herself to mend everything but she didn't know what, anything she did or said just made it worse.

Her hands were sticky with the remains of the sandwich, which felt disgusting, so when the letters fell to the floor and made her jump out of her trance, the first thing she did was get rid of the sandwich. With an apologetic glance at her mother's bent back, she threw it into the kitchen bin. She dried her hands on a towel, a hasty process that left bits of grated cheese stuck to the material, but she didn't notice, she was too busy grabbing the rest of the sandwiches, which she was glad to find were still in their individually wrapped cling film packets. Carefully she turned the picnic box upright and placed it back onto the table, then she cautiously stole a glance at Lorna, who was shuddering slightly, but still not saying anything. Cassie stretched one arm towards her, as if she were going to pat her mother's shoulder, but the arm wavered in the air, she didn't dare touch her mum in case the sobbing got louder. She waited for a moment, then dropped her hand and began to pick up the rest of the items. There weren't many, so they were soon packed into the picnic box. There was nothing else she could do, and she was worried about dad getting back and finding them like this, so she bent down and crept nearer to her mother.

"You okay, mum?" she ventured. Lorna kept her hands over her eyes and blew a huge sigh in reply.

"No Cass, I'm not." Cassie looked away, distressed, and spotted two apples which had rolled under the table. She retrieved them, then went back and crouched down on her knees next to her mum, trying to prise the hands away from the face. Lorna was determined that she didn't want to let go of her grip, and pushed her hands harder against her face; Cassie was terrified.

"Mum, please, Dad'll be back soon." She said, and with those words Lorna's strength disappeared; her hands fell limply to her sides. Now, when Cassie could see the wet cheeks and silent shuddering, she wished she hadn't tried to help. 'I'm making it worse,' she kept thinking, 'every time I do something, I end up making it worse. I'm so stupid'. Awkwardly she stood up and found the tissues, and then began clumsily dabbing at her mother's tears, but the act seemed to irritate Lorna. Roughly, she pushed Cassie away, and began chiding herself bitterly as she compelled her body to stand up.

"Silly me, silly me!" she muttered, jabbing herself in the face with the tissues and blowing her nose loudly. She looked at her daughter, she seemed to want to say something meaningful, her eyes were large, teary and expressive. It looked like her mum was asking her for something *and* telling her something at the same time. There was a message in there somewhere, but Cassie didn't know what. Cassie stared at Lorna helplessly.

"What is it, mum?" she asked quietly, but that was the wrong thing to say. Already her mum's eyes were changing. The pupils were closing, the irises darkening, the appearance was becoming much more severe, and then Lorna was speaking again, in a false, brittle voice.

"I don't know what's wrong with me. Fancy getting so upset." She spoke angrily, but who Lorna was directing the anger at, Cassie wasn't sure. 'It must be me, for spilling the picnic,' she thought, and her eyes began instantly welling up with tears.

"No!" Lorna said harshly, when she saw Cassie's face starting to wobble. Lorna was forcing herself to smile, but her teeth were gritted, and her lips could barely support the movement. The smile was faltering, even Cassie could see it, but her mother's determination won through.

"'Don't cry over spilt picnics' – that should be my motto!" she said, throwing down the joke as if it were a gauntlet. For a moment there was silence between them and then Cassie made herself laugh, as she knew she was expected to. It was a hollow attempt, stopping almost as soon as she had begun, but it was enough. Lorna dropped her guard and relaxed a little. Now the strength of her determination had left her, she drooped, and was sad again. Silently they both packed the rest of the picnic together, Cassie going to the cupboard without instruction, hoping she was getting the right items, but too aware of the delicate equilibrium to ask. Her mother was too miserable to care. The spell was only broken when Cassie's dad returned. He had wheeled himself back from the shops successfully, and manoeuvred through the front door exhilarated with the exercise and his independence. He noticed Cassie's unhappy face straightaway, and sensed the atmosphere in the silence and for one moment he hesitated, but a little of the old Mike had returned with the freedom of being out on his own, so instead of being overcome with depression himself, he immediately decided to tease them out of it, and harangue them into a better mood. He pushed himself briskly forward to join them.

"Hi guys, I'm home," he called out cheerfully; wheeling into the dining room. Stopping the wheelchair just in front of Cassie, Mike changed his voice dramatically. "Good grief my wheels are stuck! What's all this?" Lorna rushed through from the kitchen, where she had disappeared to finish the dishes, so that her husband would not see her tears. She was wiping her hands on a tea towel and peering at the bottom of the wheelchair in puzzlement.

"There's nothing there," she said slowly.

"Well fancy that! It must have been your chins I got stuck on, your faces were so long!" Lorna looked at him in amazement, then burst out into surprised laughter. Mike was thrilled.

"Now that's better," he smiled, "don't you agree Cass?" Cassie nodded silently, sidling up to her father to link her hand in his and stand by him.

"You haven't teased me in ages," Lorna observed. The tears were still wet on her cheeks, but her eyes glittered again with some of their old sparkle. "You used to be dreadful."

"Oh I used to be dreadful, did I? That's a nice thing to say about your old dad, isn't it Cass?"

"Mum was just joking, dad," Cassie answered anxiously, her eyes filling with tears.

"Heyyy! I know that, don't be so sensitive," Mike said quickly, pulling Cassie to his shoulder for a cuddle and exchanging a worried look with Lorna, which their daughter fortunately did not see.

"Who's ready for a trip then?" he prompted, hoping to distract Cassie out of her solemn spirits. "It's a glorious day, mustn't waste it!"

"Yes, we're ready. Cassie helped me get the picnic together, didn't you, love?" her mum remarked casually. Cassie, reminded of her clumsiness, nodded slowly, her eyes round and glassy with tears restrained.

"Off we go, then, I'll get the picnic!" Mike announced cheerily; gritting his teeth with determination as he headed forward and grabbed the picnic from the table. He'd always carried the picnics before the accident, usually striding forward discussing politics with Lizzie, disregarding the heavy rucksack on his back. On warm days lunch was carried in a coolbox, heavy and cumbersome, which he swung effortlessly on the way down to the beach, or whichever destination Lorna had organised; usually somewhere with a long walk attached. Today he didn't even try to think it through, he couldn't bear to, as far as he was concerned he'd *always* carried the box, and he would again. This was the first picnic since the accident, and Lorna had packed everything without thinking. Out of habit she had pulled out the largest picnic box and automatically filled it with enough food for four. She had given no thought at all to the practicalities of carrying it; now she bitterly regretted her hasty decision. She watched hopelessly, as Mike grabbed the cumbersome box and perched it resolutely on his knee. He balanced the burden with one hand while manoeuvring out of the house with the other. His only admission that the action was anything other than effortless, came in the form of an escaping grunt. Progress was slow and laboured; with the box to unbalance him, Mike took ages simply to get from one room to another. Cassie and Lorna followed slowly as the procession moved through the house, their hands useless by their sides, as Mike's pride refused to let them do anything at all to help. Lorna was desperately trying to stop herself from mentally calculating how much time they would save, if she snatched the box off Mike's knee and let Cassie carry it, while she pushed the wheelchair quickly through to the door and outside. Cassie was struggling to contain her restless energy and eagerness to set off. Instead, they both hovered helplessly behind the wheelchair, mute and nearly immobile, in a painful pretence that nothing was wrong.

Chapter 12

Once installed in his specially adapted car, and out of the hated wheelchair, Mike came into his own. From the outside the car looked perfectly normal and so did Mike. Knowing that no one could possibly see his disability gave him his old confidence back. He sat tall and grasped the wheel firmly, holding his life in his hands, literally. Blood pumped straight to his finger-tips, and his heart raced faster, until the thump of the beats threatened to burst from his chest. Just turning the ignition key set his nerves on fire, and his breath started to come out in gasps. He sounded like Cassie imagined a drowning man would sound, one who had only just been able to get to the surface, suddenly, for air, after nearly dying, and each sharp, painful lungful of air was taking him one step nearer to life. The desperation alarmed Cassie. She was *always* terrified when she was in the car with her father, and she was sure her mother felt the same way. She had seen the white clenched hand, gripping the side of the passenger seat in front, down by the door where her father couldn't see. Then, there was the silence. Neither of them ever spoke a word in the car. Even if Mike asked a question, no-one ever answered. It didn't matter to him; he remained happily oblivious, gripping the wheel and grinning, addressing no one in particular with his former lively banter. All their journeys passed too fast for him.

Her dad knew the way to Oakwell Hall; he and mum had evidently discussed their destination. Cassie found this comforting; it made hers seem like a normal family. Turning off the main road her dad swung the car swiftly round and down, past a couple of ponies plodding along. Hearing the car, the riders turned their faces to sneer superciliously at its passengers, but the desired effect was overshadowed by the glare of the fluorescent tabards they wore. Cassie shrank into her seat with her stomach somersaulting as she recognised Savannah. Thankfully, Savannah hadn't spotted Cassie hiding in the back of the vehicle, she was far too busy holding her head up and keeping her nose in the air, making sure that she appeared sufficiently aloof. Cassie was able to steal a glance at the fluorescent yellow tabard that Savannah wore, which had emblazoned across it

'EXTREME CAUTION, YOUNG ANIMAL.'

The thought of Savannah wearing the tabard to school, and the look that would appear on Jason's face, made Cassie smile slightly just at the moment when her mum looked round, white-faced, to whisper 'we're here'. Lorna's evident surprise was quickly replaced by a genuine beam of pleasure.

"I knew you'd like it here, Cass. Didn't I say, Mike?"

"You certainly did, love." Mike replied, glancing into the rear-view mirror to see Cassie's smile, which broadened considerably when she realised the car had pulled into a car park, and her dad was just parking it. She jumped eagerly out and looked around. They had stopped in a corner where the sandy gravel was particularly dusty. There were designated disabled parking places, but her father had driven past them. It would be harder for her mother to push his chair from this recess, but Cassie knew Lorna would rather do battle with the stones than her husband's motives.

Edging the car park in front of her was a shadowy avenue of trees, sheltering the drive to the house. They looked spooky even in daylight, Cassie decided, the heavy canopy of leaves roused by the breeze into creating apparitions among the tree trunks below. To her right were low, sunny buildings, made of warm welcoming stone and situated in a pleasant courtyard, but these were not Oakwell Hall. The Hall itself stood alone, dark and menacing, beyond the ghostly avenue. Peering across through the trees and the tourists, Cassie was struck by the funereal aspect of the building. The stone was almost black with age, the windows were dulled with antique glass and moss shrouded the damp surface, as Cassie had seen it do on old gravestones. She shivered involuntarily, even though it was a hot day, and turned back to her parents.

Lorna had just succeeded in getting Mike out of the car and settled into his wheelchair. In changing vehicles he had changed persona; just now, in the aftermath of the awkward struggle, he was a shrunken elderly man, his bitter expression effectively repudiating assistance, even before it was offered. Other visitors looked guiltily away as they passed Lorna labouring with the wheelchair, making Mike both irritated and relieved at the same time. Once they cleared the difficult, dusty corner, and the wheels began to move more freely, his features relaxed. Cassie joined them and the three of them set off up the car park, determined to be an ordinary family enjoying an ordinary day out.

★　★　★

Leaving the sandy gravel and gaining a firmer path which swung into the sunny courtyard, Cassie and her mum naturally meandered there first. There was a gift shop on their left.

"You're in there last, if at all, girls!" Mike ordered, smiling.

"Oh, what's that?" Cassie asked, pointing towards brightly decorated doors in front of them.

"Let's go and see, shall we?" Lorna replied, pleased at Cassie's enthusiasm. Her daughter slipped ahead, lively as a lamb, disappearing through the entrance, but then she remembered and came back to dutifully hold the door, so that it was easier for Lorna to get the wheelchair through.

They all liked the Discovery Centre. Apart from one slope, where Lorna had to push Mike, he was able to get himself about easily, so he felt comfortable, and for Cassie there were exhibits to explore and a slide. Lorna loved seeing Cassie so happy. She often felt struck with guilt that they did not get out as much as they had before the accident, but without Lizzie... and then there was Mike's chair to consider. Still, they were out now, that was the main thing. Resolving to give Cassie as much attention as possible, Lorna bent down with her, peering into holes and sliding little circles of wood about, which gave her the names of bird models hanging above. At first she felt faintly foolish, but soon she was enjoying herself too much to care. Mike watched them, gratified, and even allowed himself to turn a prism to make a rainbow, when the other visitors were out of sight. He called Cassie to stand next to him. She was enthralled by the colours, standing spellbound as her father heaved at the wheel.

"At least all this arm exercise is good for something!" he joked, without bitterness, as he turned the glass through the light, the colours flashing quicker and quicker until they both laughed out loud. As they left the centre and went out of the courtyard, the family were more relaxed than they had been all year. For the first time in months Lorna was feeling guilt free about Cassie, and Mike was chattering away to his daughter about what he'd seen. 'Just like a normal family,' Lorna thought, smiling at the back of Mike's head, as she pushed him towards the Hall.

Chapter 13

As they approached the gothic mansion, the family automatically fell silent. On the large lawn in front of the house two toddlers ran, their parents close behind, but their shouts seemed oddly muffled. The harsh grating that the wheelchair was making on the gravelled path was crushing their happy mood, already the day seemed a little less sunny. Cassie was grateful when the noise stopped, 'footsteps on gravel never sound like that' she was thinking, but managed to stop herself from uttering the thought aloud. She stole a guilty glance at her father, as if he could read her mind, but he was morosely glaring at the appearance of two steps, the first of which had necessitated the sudden halt.

"Oh. There's a couple of steps," Lorna remarked, trying to sound casual. "I never thought of that. Still, I can soon get you up there." She quickly lurched the chair back to lift the front wheels onto the first step, and then, tilting the chair forward again, triumphantly manoeuvred the wheels up the stone path. Another step awaited them to get into the house, "Easy Peasy." Lorna announced, determined to hold on to the pleasant mood they had been sharing. She pushed Mike forward and gestured with her free hand for Cassie to go in front, to open the great wooden door before them. It was too heavy really for Cassie, but she struggled valiantly while her father looked on blankly. He was trying not to think of how different things could have been, but still in his mind he saw the vision of himself before the accident: striding forwards boldly, confidently leading his family; Lizzie by his side, Cassie and her mum usually dawdling behind, both easily distracted into daydreams. Mike had always been impatient, wanting to rush ahead and get on, but Lizzie calmed him, made him laugh. Lizzie always understood.

Lizzie *had* always understood, he corrected himself. *Had.*

Just thinking of that word forced his face to twist in pain and he turned his head away, hiding his wretched expression behind his right hand, and squeezing the bridge of his nose between his finger and thumb, hoping that he could stem the flow of emotions in the same way that some people stopped nosebleeds. Lorna had noticed the sudden motion and would have bent down to inspect him, but suddenly the door closed behind them with a delayed, deadened thud, and they were plunged into darkness, swallowed up by the black hole which was the entrance to the Oakwell Hall.

The family waited in silence, confused and disorientated. They were temporarily blinded by the switch from sunshine to shade. As their eyes gradually adjusted, Lorna realised that there was an opening into the main hall, and she carefully turned the wheelchair into that room. Slowly they entered, awed by the polished wood panels clothing every surface. The room was completely silent. At first, Cassie thought they were quite alone but gradually, almost as if some ghostly manifestation had materialised into the room with them, she became aware that there was a man seated not three feet away, his head bent, he was peering into a book. Startled, she quickly clutched at her mother's sleeve, but then, as her vision cleared, she noticed that this 'phantom' read a paperback Jeffrey Archer. Instantly Cassie realised that he must be an attendant, if a rather quiet one, and at once she relaxed. Smiling at her own silliness, Cassie went off to look round. She was instantly drawn to the long table at the opposite side of the room. Going closer, Cassie was delighted to see that it was set with ancient writing materials, excitedly she called back to her parents.

"Look Mum, quill pens! We had these at school."

"Lovely, let's have a look then," Lorna replied, pushing the chair forward in the direction of the table.

"Don't touch!!!" A voice boomed suddenly, shattering the silence. Mike turned round sharply, angered by the sudden accusation, but the attendant was not even looking at the family, his head was buried innocently in the book, as if he had never spoken. Mike was forced to content himself with grumbling loudly.

"Shouldn't leave things out if they're that delicate, careful you don't breathe near it Cass, wouldn't want the paper disintegrating." Cassie had backed away from the table at the first shout and now looked nervously at her parents, but they smiled encouragingly, so she wandered over to the fireplace, looking dutifully, but without much interest, at the picture above it.

"Can we go into another room, Mum?" Cassie asked, eager to be out of the sombre hall.

"Of course we can, love. You lead the way." Lorna replied, trying to appear cheerful. In reality she was as anxious as Cassie to move on. She started to chew her bottom lip again, she wanted desperately to enjoy their day together.

"I'm afraid not." The voice boomed again.

"Sorry, what did you say?" Mike growled, his astonishment was giving way to anger.

"I meant *unfortunately* you cannot go any further." The attendant answered, looking up from his book directly at Mike, who met his gaze defiantly. "Regrettably there is no wheelchair access to the rest of the house." As soon as he had finished speaking, the man dropped his head down quickly. Mike continued to stare at him but remained silent, he was angry, but he felt he had no where to direct the anger to; no matter how rude that man had been, it wasn't *his* fault that Mike was in a wheelchair. Mike didn't consider other possibilities, or reasons why his anger might be justified, instead he let his fury fall inwards. Lorna stood behind him, feeling helpless. She was clutching the handles of the wheelchair as if she were drowning and they were the only life raft. Her knuckles were white. Beneath the surface of her usual quiet composure, vast oceans of emotion were seething. She watched her husband's shoulders slouch, his dignity and self respect swept away, she saw her daughter's disappointed face, such a contrast to the happy one which had been a joy to look at just fifteen minutes ago, and something in Lorna burst. Furiously she yanked the wheelchair round, almost tipping Mike onto the polished floor, and alarming the attendant who feared for the furniture.

"I've bought tickets to come here today. Nothing was said at the shop."

"But Mum, dad didn't go in with you," Cassie reminded her, trying to be helpful. Lorna glared at Cassie, trying to contain her swirling emotions, and *not* take her anger out on her daughter. Mike stayed silent, slumped immobile before her.

"We want our money back." She announced, the slight

111

waver in her voice the only indication of the turbulence within. Beneath her only-just-civil exterior a battle was being fought: a ferocious rage sought to burst through her resolution to remain as calm as possible. The fury of this long-repressed, unacknowledged anger was becoming too powerful for her to contain for much longer. She was fighting to control it for the sake of Mike and Cassandra. A burning sensation of bile rose in her throat but she swallowed it back down with difficulty, determined to force the bitterness back into the depths.

"But, Madam," began the attendant,

"NOW!" Cassie's mum shouted, her voice louder than it had been for months; the command resonated round the walls. The Jeffrey Archer was dropped and the man scuttled off in search of someone else, muttering under his breath, glancing fearfully in Lorna's direction as he went. Mike looked up at Lorna and grinned.

"Hey! You soon saw him off! What a turkey! That quite cheered me up, seeing him run like that."

"Well I'm glad to hear it." Lorna smiled grimly, staring down at her rigid hands, the knucklebones showing through. Cassie could easily recognise that Lorna was not happy, but what could she say? She opened her mouth to ask if her mum was all right, but Lorna must have anticipated the question, because she quickly switched to her 'bright, cheerful' mode: lifting her head to smile challengingly at Cassie with that familiar, forced grimace.

"Well Cassie, that was quite a performance, don't you think? I never knew I had it in me!"

"Very impressive mum," Cassie agreed. "What will you do for the second half, yell at his boss too?"

"Don't be so cheeky!" Her mother said hollowly,

forcing herself to laugh a laugh of nervous relief, so that Cassie would think she was having fun, although Cassie wasn't fooled one bit. "Now why don't you have a wander round? No need for us all to stand here. We'll be outside when you've finished. I saw an ice cream van out there, that'll keep your dad happy!"

"I'm not a kid you know!" Mike protested sulkily.

"So you don't want one then?" Lorna teased.

"I didn't say that!" Mike answered quickly, but he was smiling again at Lorna, who looked down at him fondly then bent to kiss his cheek. Mike's hand clutched at his wife's arm, holding Lorna to him greedily. They remained there, comforting each other. Nothing was said, but Cassie felt suddenly left out.

"I'll go for a look round then," she muttered, to no one in particular, and turned to leave the room without waiting for a reply.

Chapter 14

Through the doorway at the other end of the hall there were steps and a room to the left, a notice described it as a parlour. Cassie looked about briefly, she found it prettily arranged, but with a stuffy atmosphere. She could still hear her parents in the Hall, their voices were muffled, but Cassie could sense rising agitation in her mum's voice now that the bravado was fading. She could tell that Lorna was embarrassed and no doubt regretted having committed that most terrible of sins – "causing a scene". Cassie left the parlour hastily to go out of ear shot, moving quickly but quietly up the stairs, and entering a bedroom on the left as she reached the top.

Now the house was silent, her parents' voices were absorbed into the ancient woodwork, and Cassie felt more relaxed. She liked the airy bedroom, with the huge old bed taking pride of place. She stood facing unusual windows: big apertures not filled with a single pane of glass but with a multitude of small diamond-shaped pieces. The light which came through them was different, it had been fragmented until it shimmered, so that the air in the room seemed to quiver in expectation of something. As Cassie took her stance carefully behind the wooden barriers and leaned forward towards the bed, from the corner of her eye a sudden glimmer caught her attention. For the first time, she noticed a sword left in the room, placed in readiness against a table. She stared at it for a long time. There seemed to be a succession of scattering, fleeting pictures reflected across the sword's shining surface, a series of flickering patterns, not unlike a Victorian magic lantern show she'd once seen with Lizzie.

She watched for some time, until a motion through the window drew her attention away. There was no one out there, the movement she had seen must just have been the sun coming through the trees. *The trees.* Cassie looked again at the trees, what was different about them? It looked like they had shrunk! Perhaps they seemed smaller because they were being flung about in a breeze, which had sprung up quite violently. She looked down to the avenue which bordered the drive, to see if her parents were bothered by the sudden wind, but they were not there, only someone in peculiar old fashioned costume. Someone dressed as the master of the house for the sake of the visitors, she presumed. He was heavily over-acting, dragging one leg as if to pretend he had come home from a long day at the battle. She watched as the man made his way slowly through the avenue of trees, dropping objects as he went. Someone's going to have to pick all that up, Cassie thought, and then she spotted a soft figure emerge, presumably from the house, and go running, exactly as a maid would have done, to meet the master and gather the helmet and the cloak he had discarded. It was all very convincing. The two came up to the house and Cassie heard the door slam sharply, not heavily like it had done when she had entered with her parents. Then there was the sound of commotion downstairs. It must be the attendant saying something, or perhaps the man was greeting her parents. Cassie hoped that her mum and dad had a good view, both Master and Maid must have walked right in front

115

of them. She could hear the ringing of the metal spurs as the man in costume walked across the polished floor of the hall. What will the attendant think of that? She grinned, and then she began to panic a little as she heard the heavy tread stomping up the stairs. To her astonishment he came right into the bedroom in which Cassie was still standing, immobile, as if she was in a trance. He rudely shoved past her without greeting her, or even appearing to notice her presence, 'probably because I'm a child' Cassie thought bitterly, and then he flung his boots in one corner before propping the sword up carefully within reach. The maid scurried after, she too ignored Cassie as she hurried after the master, hastily trying to clean up the mud and bloody footprints. Gosh it was a mess, and yet it was very clever how everything appeared so authentic; Cassie was impressed. She was about to say something to the two actors when a rush of *real* footsteps up the stairs dispelled the image, and once again the room was back as it was, empty except for Cassie.

It was a shock, she felt as if someone had hit her in the stomach. 'I must have been daydreaming again,' she thought, but before she could wonder or think of anything else the loud exclamations of two small boys who had entered the room interrupted her thoughts.

"Eergh! Mam, mam look a sword!" the older child shrieked, pointing a chocolate covered finger in the general direction of the table.

"A thord!" lisped the younger child, who was looking at his brother for approval, copying the gesture with an equally sticky finger. Their mother wheezed an inaudible reply as she came into the room after them. She was a large woman and puffed heavily from the climb up the stairs, she caught her breath long enough to nod in northern civility at Cassie.

"Morning." Cassie smiled shyly, still a little shocked. "Hello."

"What's that, mam?" asked the older boy, pointing to a chamber pot on the floor next to the bed.

"Why, you know what that is, our Ryan," the mother panted, "t'aint so long since I got yer Granny to give hers up!" Ryan sniggered and then as his mother turned to look about the room, he knelt down to his younger brother and whispered in his ear.

"Maaam!" screamed the small boy instantly. "Our Ryan says there's wee wee in that pot an' it's off a dead man!"

"Jake! Honestly!" the mother admonished, exasperated, taking both boys rapidly out of the room with an embarrassed glance at Cassie. Cassie lingered in the bedroom; the children's excited voices in the rooms beyond were soon muffled by the thick air, so that she waited in silence. Minutes passed and she remained expectant, surveying the objects arranged about, staring across at the view through the myriad of miniature panes, searching among the figures filtering through the avenue for a familiar outline. There were plenty of people about now, and no wind at all, in fact it was sunny and warm, not a trace of the earlier bluster. Cassie easily spotted her parents at the ice cream van, and she smiled indulgently at them, yet her eye roved restlessly on. Finally, barely conscious that a decision to move had been made, she meandered into the next corridor. The ancient wood beneath her creaked and she had the illusion of the floor swaying, making her nauseous. She turned to go through the next bedroom, nearly colliding with a middle aged couple and their teenage son who were discussing the merits of the ornate bed cover. Pushing past them, desperate for some fresh air, she found herself on the balcony overlooking the main hall where she had entered with her parents. Downstairs the room was again empty, except for the attendant, who ignored her, although she was sure he knew she was there. She followed Ryan and Jake, who were sliding their hands along the top of the rail with an annoying squeak of skin against wood. As Ryan drew level with the chandelier hanging from the roof, he leapt out to grab it, drawing a warning hiss from his mother, but, Cassie noticed, not even a glance from the attendant.

A quick peep into the other upstairs rooms sufficed for Cassie and she went downstairs, still following the mother with her two boys. Ryan soon disappeared under the dividing rope in the hall, Jake close behind, right in front of the attendant, who still didn't look up from his book, until the woman following got stuck trying to keep up with her sons. Finally, he rose to his feet, putting the precious paperback down, muttering under his breath about unruly, uncontrollable children to the great distress of the beleaguered parent, who was eventually released, red-faced and harassed, to set off in hot pursuit of the two miscreants. Cassie watched them go, then started to go through the doorway into the last room of the house, the dining room, but she stopped suddenly when she realised there were people in there already. Two girls sat at the end of the long table, in the corner furthest from the doorway. They were thoroughly absorbed in some activity, aided by a kindly faced woman who stood between their seats and quietly murmured encouragement, occasionally educating by example. Cassie was struck by the brightness of their clothing, in contrast to the dreary surroundings of the dark panelling. Both girls wore yellow shirts beneath bright floral pinafores and their teacher was attired in a brilliant orange blouse. A sudden shaft of sunlight, entering from the adjacent window, illuminated the scene with all the radiance of a biblical vision, and Cassie was overwhelmed. She turned to leave quietly without disturbing the peaceful group, when she realised that someone else had noiselessly entered the room and now stood next to her. It was the girl she had thought was Charlotte Brontë, who had preferred the name Talli, and Cassie immediately realised that she had been expecting her. This was the familiar outline her eye had been striving to find when she had paused in the upstairs bedroom. Cassie stared at Talli, she knew there was no pretence this time, she couldn't possibly imagine that Talli was a real person dressed up, she had materialised out of nowhere. Cassie was nervous, but pleased to see her again, she had questions she wanted to ask her. Yet Cassie still stood without speaking, looking pleased and puzzled all at the same time, so that it was a smiling Talli that broke the silence, her expressive eyes saying much to reassure Cassie, while nodding her head at the three in the corner, a casual comment fell from her lips.

"It's a fine sight to see schoolgirls so happily employed; she's an excellent woman, Mrs Cockill, like a mother to her pupils."

"You know her then?" Cassie asked, surprised.

"Of course, I've visited here often. It's quite a gothic old barrack on the outside, but that makes it all the more fascinating to see how vibrant are the people who reside *inside*. This group has a lovely atmosphere, for example even their clothing is colourful. It's just the sort of school I'd like to run with my sisters when we're older, you can imagine the fun we'd have!" She waved her hand in the direction of the teacher and her pupils, her eyes alight with enthusiasm, "Their attire is a delightful contrast to the drab uniforms I had to wear at my first school, but that was pretty dreadful all round." She paused, and added sadly, "My older sisters died after they went there." Cassie had been nodding animatedly while Talli had been talking but at the final sentence her face had fallen and she had looked away, gulping back a tear. Talli instantly stopped talking and peered closely at Cassie. Glancing out of the room quickly, she then took Cassie's hand in her own, and led her out of a door at the back of the house. Outside, Talli rushed Cassie across a lawn and up a flight of steps to a terraced garden. There were a few couples walking round, admiring the neatly trimmed hedges and flowerbeds, but Talli pulled Cassie past them and the two girls went noisily crunching down the gravel path to the very end of the garden, where there were no visitors to the quiet rose beds. The flower borders were sheltered, within high stone walls adorned with climbing fruit trees, and in the middle of them was one solitary bench, which looked back down towards the house. Talli headed straight for it and gestured Cassie to sit down. Then, pushing her skirts impatiently to one side, Talli lowered herself down on to the bench next to her and waited in silence, until Cassie got her breath back.

Chapter 15

The scent of the summer surrounded them: the perfume of roses in full bloom, the sharp sweet smell of freshly cut grass wafting across from the fields, and the gentle fragrance of honeysuckle lazily drifting down from a trailing vine behind. The air was balmy after the chilly atmosphere of the house and the sun shone warmly into their sanctuary. The two figures sat quite alone, no other visitors ventured near. The only indicators that time had *not* stood still were the butterflies and bees flitting from flower to flower. Cassie followed their movements while her eyes swam with liquid. The various colours fluttered purposefully, ceaselessly, between plants; she couldn't help thinking, as she watched them, that life went on for these creatures regardless of what had happened to her and her family. Many insects passed in front of her before she finally felt able to speak. Talli had been sitting facing forward, looking down at the rear façade of Oakwell Hall, but as Cassie began to talk, she turned her inquisitive eyes to look searchingly into Cassie's face.

"I'm sorry. I didn't mean to go all, erm, what's the word... mushy." Talli was not familiar with the word, but she guessed its meaning and nodded encouragingly.

"Yes, go on." She said to Cassie, who tried to smile, but couldn't. She started to talk again, slowly.

"You startled me a little, I guess. When you spoke about your sisters, and the awful school, and what happened. It's just..." but Cassie couldn't go on. Talli was sympathetic. "Can you make it out?" she asked, but then as Cassie looked puzzled, she added, "Sorry, my friend Mary always says that to me. Can you speak about it?"

"I suppose so, I just don't try. We never talk about her at home." She paused, and took a deep breath; finally she spoke haltingly and with much trepidation.

"My sister...Lizzie... she ...died.... nine months ago." Talli nodded, sympathetically. "Well then, that's probably why I can talk to you."

"What on earth are you talking about?" Cassie replied, bewildered. She wasn't sure what reply she had expected to her words, but it certainly wasn't any of the usual responses to such an announcement. If she dared mention anything about her sister at all, which she had done less and less as time went on, the most common reaction was a long awkward silence. Sometimes, this was followed by sympathetic, meaningless murmers or shocked outrage, but after that was always, *without failure*, a swift and complete change of subject. Talli's comment was utterly unpredictable.

"I mean of course that *that* must be the link. We must have a reason to communicate across time." Talli answered matter-of-factly, Cassie stared incredulously.

"Across time?" she repeated dumbly.

"Don't be such a fool!" Talli reproved, exasperated. "It's obvious we're from completely different centuries. I thought you knew that."

"Well," Cassie pondered slowly, "I suppose I did, deep down, it's just talking of it makes it seem so incredible." She shook her head, gently, then focused her gaze on the darkened edifice of Oakwell Hall.

"I always knew I had a fiery imagination." Talli smiled,

"Am I imagining you now?"

"Surely it's me inventing you!" Cassie laughed. "I'm always getting told off for daydreaming."

"That could be the link, then. Vivid dreams. Maybe our brains are both the same – and different to everyone else's!"

"Oh, don't tell me, I know. Mum's favourite piece of science. 'We only use ten percent of our brains in everyday thinking!"

"Really?" Talli was immediately intrigued. "How do they know?"

"Don't ask me! My mum knows. She told me all about it once, but I've forgotten."

"Your mother spoke to you, and you don't remember?" It was Talli's turn now to look crestfallen.

"Not a crime is it?" Cassie replied flippantly, but then immediately regretted it when she saw how distressed her companion had become.

"I'm sorry. What did I say?" she asked concerned.

"My mother died when I was young, I barely remember her." Talli replied simply.

"I'm sorry," Cassie echoed, now she was the one feeling awkward.

"I told you I lost both my older sisters through going to a certain school." Talli continued. "Your sister, was she older than you?"

"Oh, yes. Older, and much, much cleverer. She was an amazing reader. She read the paper with dad from being really young. She got on so well with him, he feels it terribly. We all do."

"My eldest sister, Maria, was the same, she had this remarkable intellect and she was full of wisdom. It made her really mild and yet she had such an inner strength. I

123

always felt no one else could notice me when she was around."

"Your sister, Maria?" Cassie paused for a moment, thinking. "I remember someone telling me something about her. You say she was very clever?"

"The most talented of us all, easily."

"But I heard she got into trouble at school. Was she badly behaved?" Cassie asked bluntly. Talli looked horrified at the question.

"No, never. She was like an angel. But there was one teacher who didn't like her, said she was.." she hesitated, she hated using the word even now, "*Slatternly*. She punished Maria severely, cruelly I would say, but Maria never complained. She always accepted her 'faults', as she called them!" Talli raged angrily, her face bitter with the vehemence of her memories. "Unable to be subjected to systematic arrangements!" What sort of a defect is that?" Cassie suddenly remembered the woman at the Parsonage.

"Your sister Maria! She was a daydreamer, I remember that lady in costume that day, the one we thought was your mum, but she was meant to be your Aunt Branwell. She said Maria went to some really awful school, she was going to tell us what happened to her but she went, and we never saw her again."

"No, that's right. We never saw her again," Talli murmured sadly. Cassie looked at her, puzzled.

"I meant we never saw your Aunt again, that day at the Museum."

"Oh, I thought you meant Maria. We never saw her again. Elizabeth, Emily and I were at school with her but she became very ill. One day Papa came to collect her and took her away. For nights afterward I laid awake wondering if she was alive or dead. I used to dream she was next to me so I could keep her warm; she was always shivering at school. They told me later that she died at home, with Papa and Aunt Branwell to care for her, but we didn't get to say goodbye."

"I didn't get to say goodbye either." Cassie blurted out resentfully; she shocked herself at the bitterness that came out with the words. She looked at Talli, trying to gauge her reaction, but Talli was silent, waiting for her to continue, so she carried on, more slowly.

"My sister died in hospital, covered in tubes. I was in a different ward. Mum and dad didn't want me to see her like that. They wanted me to remember her how she was *before* the accident. I do remember that, but it makes it harder to understand why she died, going from being so alive, to just..." Cassie's voice trailed off sadly. Both girls remained silent, their faces turned downward, but just then, a warm breeze wafted gently across their shoulders like a comforting caress. As if in response to it, Cassie lifted her head and spoke first.

"It's been nice to talk about Lizzie," she said slowly. "No one talks about her at home."

"People react to grief differently," Talli said thoughtfully.

"What did you do?" Cassie asked, looking hopefully into Talli's face.

"That was our Secret."

"Oh." Cassie looked downcast, Talli patted her hand affectionately and suddenly smiled so that her whole demeanour changed. The sadness melted away and her face glowed vibrantly. It was like the sun had appeared from behind a cloud and suffused Talli with its warm rays.

"I mean we had our Secret: '*Scribblemania*'."

"*Scribble Mania*? What's that?" Cassie asked automatically, fascinated by Talli's sudden change in appearance, scarcely even thinking about the peculiarity of the name of her subject.

"It's something we all suffered from, and it was our cure for everything." Talli laughed. "*When you are going to write because you just cannot help it! Scribblemania was just a name someone called it once.*"

"How would that help then?" Cassie wondered, thinking of all the pages she struggled to complete at school. Mostly, teachers only seemed concerned with grammar, spelling and appearance. Her parents looked at it from time to time, flicking through and glancing at the teachers' comments; always negative ones about the state of her handwriting. She could hardly begin to write down all her innermost feelings in there, Mrs Harrison would have a fit!

"You've heard of Robert Southey?" Talli asked.

"No, not at all." Cassie replied, bemused. Talli allowed herself a half smile. "And yet you're studying my family at school? In my day Robert Southey was the Poet Laureate and one of the most eminent writers in the land. Once, when I was twenty, I actually dared to send a letter to him along with some of my poems. It was a rather foolish letter, I see now, wildly enthusiastic, and he was rather shocked. He warned me against my daydreams and told me that '*Literature cannot be the business of a woman's life*'."

"He told you to stop writing, just because you were a woman?" Cassie asked incredulously. Talli laughed at her horror struck face.

"He didn't say that I should stop *totally*, merely that I

should not aim for celebrity. He suggested that I ought to spend more time in the real world instead of indulging in daydreams."

"Did he think daydreams were bad?" Cassie asked eagerly.

"He thought they would induce a *'distempered state of mind'*" Talli said, in a mock pompous voice which made both girls laugh.

"What could you do instead?"

"I had to occupy myself with *'proper duties'*."

"'Proper duties?'" Cassie asked, puzzled.

"Domestic ones, looking after a house and family."

"But you didn't follow his advice."

"Yes, I did, and I was grateful for Mr Southey's words, although I confess, I was a little disappointed at first."

"But you must have carried on, you're more famous than he is." Cassie mused. Talli smiled.

"Well, he also wrote to me that writing was, *next to religion, the surest means of soothing the mind.* That was true indeed and some years later I put it into practice."

"What happened?"

"My father was in Manchester for an eye operation and he wanted me to be in the room while it was conducted. There were no pain killing drugs such as are used these days." She paused, remembering, and a shudder went down her spine. "It had to be done, and indeed it was successful, but to aid his recovery he had to spend a month in a darkened room. I was unwell myself, I kept thinking about all that I had seen and heard, and, *worse*, smelt. I was becoming more and more anxious, and I had so much time. There were so many thoughts in my head. I was wondering if he would recover, remembering other people I had lost.... In the end I did the only thing that could take my mind away from such things, I began to write."

"What did you write?"

"I began Jane Eyre, the book that changed my whole life."

"And did it sooth your mind?" Cassie asked. Talli laughed guiltily at the question.

"At first, but then I got *so* caught up in the story, that even after we returned home I wrote incessantly for three weeks, so that I made myself ill again." It was Cassie's turn to laugh. Talli continued:

"It is Robert Southey's words that I am passing onto you, he felt that writing could be *wholesome* for the heart and soul." Talli paused for a moment, thoughtful, then became more animated. She leapt to her feet and began to pace about the gravel pathway as she spoke. "I did wonder if he ever felt the *other* effect though, how much it can agitate the mind and spirit! Poor Mr Southey was quite alarmed for my mind!" Cassie laughed again.

"But it obviously did you good! You seem perfectly sane to me."

"Yes, but if you knew my thoughts, the dreams that absorb me; and the fiery imagination that at times eats me up... That's why I wrote it all down, otherwise it would have driven me clean daft."

"So 'Scribblemania' is simply writing things down," Cassie proffered. Talli acquiesced, and was about to continue when suddenly a voice called out,

"Cassie! Cassie!" Standing up, Cassie could just see Lorna nervously entering the garden through a small gate tucked away to the left of the house.

"It's my mum, I'd better go." She said reluctantly to Talli, who nodded enthusiastically.

"Of course you must. I'd rush to meet my mother." She beamed, and, almost pushing Cassie away, sent her off down the path to meet Lorna. Such behaviour struck Cassie as odd, most people she knew found their parents a pain, she wondered if it was because of a strict upbringing in the Brontë household: Cassie's great granddad had always harked back to the Victorian method of raising children, "seen but not heard"; but then she remembered what Talli had just said, that her mother had died when she was young. Cassie had been more struck by the death of Talli's older sister Maria which had so reminded her of the death of Lizzie, that she had hardly given a thought about Talli's mother. She realised she ought to have said something, and stopped suddenly to turn back, but Talli was already gone. Wildly, Cassie looked from side to side, scanning the paths obscured by bushes, but she was hardly surprised when she saw nothing. An unexpected voice behind her made her jump.

"Looking for me?"

"Mum!!" Cassie shouted and twisting round she flung her arms around her mother, squeezing her tightly so that Lorna could scarcely breathe.

"Cass," she began, quite overcome with the close embrace and the unusually exuberant affection. "Cass, darling. Were you lost? I thought you knew where we were. I only just popped into the shop for a moment, I wouldn't have gone in if I thought you'd be panicking..."

"I wasn't lost Mum," Cassie interrupted, still hugging her mother furiously.

"Well thank goodness for that. You can let me breathe a bit you know, love, you're squashing the little booklet I got for you, all about the occupants of Oakwell Hall,

Charlotte Brontë gets a mention; apparently she used to visit here when it was a school."

"Thanks, Mum, that's great," Cassie murmured, burrowing into her mother's shoulder. Lorna began to relax a little, until Cassie's next words made her rigid again. "It's funny you should say that about Talli visiting Oakwell, I was just talking to..." Lorna's arms tensed and Cassie paused and then quickly changed her words, "I mean, thinking about Charlotte Brontë and something I'd, erm, heard about her, got me thinking. She lost her mother when she was only little and I began to wonder," She hesitated, swallowed, then continued. "What if I didn't have you. What if you'd died in the car crash instead?" Her mother gasped and clutched Cassie in shock. Cassie paused, she knew her parents hated any mention of the crash. Lorna was holding her breath now, Cassie could sense it, but she was full of her talk with Talli, exuberant lively Talli, and she ignored the warning silence. "But what if you'd been in the front seat, mum?"

"No, don't say it." Her mother checked her. "*Don't ever say it.*" She repeated, her voice dangerously low and her grip on Cassie tightened. "I'd give anything to have been in that front seat instead of her, you must know that."

"But, Mum..." Cassie began, only to find herself squeezed even harder against Lorna's shoulder, her head wedged so that she could not move her own face to see that of her mother's.

"*Don't ever, ever say it,*" her mother echoed, her voice icy. She gave her daughter one final embrace, then, loosening her grip, she stepped away and turned towards the house; she was silent while a tremor shook her body. After it had passed, still keeping her eyes averted, she hesitantly stretched out one hand in Cassie's direction. Cassie took it silently and Lorna pulled their arms together, patting Cassie's hand automatically. The two of them crunched off together across the gravel, arm in arm. An onlooker would have considered them the epitome of parental bonding, yet they walked grimly, without the solace of a single word, or one solitary shared smile.

Chapter 16

The visit was not judged to be a success and the journey home was going to be even more of a strain for Cassie and her mother. After the episode in the Hall, Mike urgently felt the need to prove himself; he quickly hauled the car rapidly out of the car park and on to the small country road. The route was too winding for such speeds; Mike found that he was accelerating fiercely out of one bend, only to be forced to brake again, almost immediately. Cassie's heart was racing; she was holding the handle of the door tightly with both hands, her face close to the glass, looking out. She would be sick if she faced inside, but as long as she focused on the features outside the car she felt better. In desperation she concentrated on the large hedges which formed a continuous sight along to the right. As they swung into the final corner, she was relieved to recognise a sign which meant they were nearly back at the main road. At the same instant a gruff shout from her father frightened her, and her knuckles turned white with the pressure of her grip.

"Jeez, look at these!" Two ponies were ambling towards them, right in the middle of the road. The riders were chatting nonchalantly and the reins hung loose over the ponies necks. An arrogant air was replaced by panic when the two girls saw how fast the car was travelling, and they grabbed the ponies' manes wildly; the brakes screeched and tyres screamed as her father swung the wheel and swerved, bringing the car to a twisted halt so that it virtually blocked the small lane. The ponies were terrified and their riders inexperienced. One animal was backing, white-eyed, away from the car and into the thorny mass of the hedge bottom; the other sidestepped toward the car, its head stretched high and the reins flapping uselessly. The young rider was clutching desperately at the animal's neck, her arms flung wide round both sides; she was making little attempt to regain control of her mount. As the pony came level with the car, Cassie found herself face to face with the rider who was looking down with fear and panic at the car and its passengers. As she recognised the outlines of the face Cassie's stomach leapt in horror: it was Savannah. To her utter misery she realised that Savannah had recognised her; it was too late to turn away. The shock of seeing Cassie spurred Savannah into action. Immediately she felt better, and was able to pick up the reins and sit back in the saddle. A smug smirk passed across Savannah's face as she jerked her pony's head round and kicked him savagely in the sides. The frightened animal cantered off up the road in panic, his hooves slipping on the hard surface. The other pony pulled itself out of the briars and followed, eager to be with its stable mate, and the riders quickly disappeared out of sight round the corner.

The family in the car watched them go in oppressive silence.

'School will be fun on Monday' Cassie thought wryly, causing a painful churning to begin deep in her stomach. She leaned forward, arms wrapped round her waist and dipped her head in an effort to relieve the tension. Lorna looked round at that moment, to check how Cassie was handling the near miss, but seeing her daughter's small, hunched figure wrenched her own feelings too much; she was forced to twist quickly forwards, and she couldn't bring herself to turn round again. The journey home was spent in a strained silence, which fostered the return of all their most harrowing memories. Mike's knuckles were white, and his face horror stricken; he appeared to think he was driving along a curved road, and kept looking first to the right and then to the left, but they had left the twisty country lane and were travelling down a virtually straight road which had high residences bordering each side. His driving was safe, but jerky; he kept his foot on the accelerator unless another car pulled out in front and then he slammed the brakes down fiercely. Only when a safe distance was achieved, enough to get a very large lorry between them and the other car at least, would the accelerator go on again, and they would surge forward quickly. Lorna was nearly sick from the motion, but her stomach was churning so much with the thoughts running through her mind, that she did not consider it travel sickness. For Cassie the sensations were even more intense. The trauma of the sudden stop, the sound of the squeal of the brakes and the sudden lurch forwards, had triggered terrible flashbacks from the night of the crash.

*   *   *

"I believe that my heart will go on..." Cassie shrieked and Lizzie howled with laughter, leaning forward from the front passenger seat of the car, she threateningly hovered one hand over the on-off button of the stereo.

"If you think you can do better than Celine, Cass," she joked warningly.

"No!!" Cassie yelled. "Don't turn it off, I love that record!"

"Yes, I know, so do I when *she* sings it!" Lizzie answered swiftly, screaming in delight as she dodged the flailing arm of her sister in the seat behind.

"Now, ladies!" Mike bellowed, in mock anger. "Stop messing about, or I'm going to pull over and haul you both out of my beautiful new baby. Isn't she wonderful? Have you noticed how quiet the engine is?"

"I'm trying to check out the stereo, dad," Lizzie replied smartly. "If we can see how quiet Cassie is!"

"Cheek!" Cassie complained good-naturedly, enjoying her sister's teasing. She remained silent though, listening to the 'Titanic' theme song. It chilled her heart as she remembered the film's scenes of heart-breaking desperation, when the people left in the icy sea struggle to survive. The stars glittered brilliantly, and silently, over the sinking ship; coldly indifferent to the tragedy unfolding beneath them. Tonight, as Cassie looked out of the window to see the skies above, there were almost as many as had been in the film. Dad had driven right out of the orange glow of the town and onto the quiet countryside roads in order to give the new car a proper test run. Cassie could see many more stars than usual, resplendently decorating the heavens, but it made her shiver to look at them, the night seemed stark and more vulnerable to the vast expanses of space, even the temperature was lower than it had been lately. Suddenly, a flash of light streaked across the firmament, disappearing even before she could speak.

"Wow! Did anyone see that?" she asked hopefully.

"What, love?" Dad answered absently, then grumbled. "Jeez, look at those lights. He must have full beam on.

You can see them right round the corner."

"Oh, that's not fair. Put it back on, Liz. I stopped singing," Cassie chided, annoyed at the abrupt cessation of the radio.

"I didn't turn it off, Cass. I was only messing about before," Lizzie answered, leaning her head forward to peer at the luminous dial. "It's still switched on." She was about to make a sarcastic remark to her younger sister, when a sharp intake of breath from their dad made her glance anxiously in his direction.

"What the...?" Mike began, staring in shocked disbelief.

They had turned the bend and were confronted with the terrible sight of a huge truck skewed between the hedgerows in front of them, entirely blocking the road. Worse, the whole truck was sliding in their direction. The brakes were screeching uselessly, the massive vehicle was locked into the movement. Mike automatically slammed his foot down on the brake pedal, but the road was covered in mud, and the car's tyres failed to grip the tarmac beneath. Mike's car was now gliding unerringly right towards the truck. Lizzie looked up to see the immense white side of the lorry looming above her. She could just make out the frantic waving of the driver, as he gestured at them to go back. Cassie hammered urgently at the back of her father's seat but to no avail, Mike was transfixed, his mouth stretched wide in a horrifying caricature of terror, with only a faint gurgle from within, as an animal waits, hypnotised, for the snake to strike.

They were all struck dumb now as the vehicles moved towards each other in agonising, inevitable motion; it was as if time had slowed, the air itself was thicker and suffocating. Cassie continued to bang rhythmically on the back of the driver's seat, but her hands moved slower, as if she were underwater. She gazed open-mouthed at the expanse of icy white as the side of the truck began to tip towards them and fall. Metal crunched, in deafening proportions, as the lorry settled on to the front of the car, crushing the bonnet and exploding the windscreen. Glass flew into the vehicle, right into Lizzie's upturned face, and then all the interior lights went out and they were engulfed in blackness.

When the two vehicles had stopped moving, Cassie sat motionless in the dark, her arms flopped by her side. They had abandoned their anxious pummelling and become inert. All she could hear was the hiss of a broken radiator and the creak of bent metal, when suddenly into the still night air, came the nervous voice of a radio DJ.

"Sorry about that folks. The radio station wishes to apologise for that break in transmission, and to assure the listeners that the technical difficulties have now been resolved and everything is, thankfully, back to normal. Hello again to all those who haven't retuned their radios..." The falsely jolly voice was suddenly drowned by the sound of terrified shrieks, hundreds of them. Cassie did not realise, until the police and paramedics arrived some time later, that it was she who had been the only one screaming; every one else was silent.

She remembered only eyes and hands and voices. Eyes and lights peering into her face, voices probing her ears, she ignored them, and remained passive while fingers opened buttons and pressed themselves gently but firmly against her skin. Once they had checked her over, and found that none of the blood on her clothes was from major injuries she had sustained, there was the tight grip as they moved her. Days later she realised she had been lifted upwards, they must have peeled back the car's roof to get to her. She wanted to ask about it, but there was no one to ask. In the ambulance, confident of her condition, they administered a sedative which stopped the awful yelling, reducing it to a troubled mumble as she fell into sleep. Her last thought, before she sank into unconsciousness, was the recognition that both her sister and her father were too quiet. To the distress of the woman paramedic travelling with her, a young mother herself, Cassie continued to mutter her concerns throughout the long journey in the back of the ambulance. Cassie cried fitfully for her sister and her father, even while her eyes were tightly shut, and her brain oblivious to the bumps and twists of the road. Outside the sky glittered with cold stars, their ancient, long travelled light still blindly twinkling, heartlessly oblivious to the drama below.

★ ★ ★

It was still night when Cassie awoke with a start in hospital; a drip attached to her arm making her feel like a prisoner. She started to scream immediately; the two low lights of the nurse's station looking vaguely like head-lamps shining through the dim ward. Two nurses came running, calling "SShhh" but the sight of strangers made Cassie even more frightened. The older nurse realised this, and sent her colleague hurrying to fetch Cassie's mother. While she waited, she pulled the curtains round the bed, and kept up a constant hum of chatter, hoping to sooth the patient, but it was to no avail. Only when

Lorna arrived, panting, out of breath, rushing from her vigil at the other side of the hospital, did Cassie stop screaming. The nurse pulled a chair right up to Cassie's bedside and Lorna sat down obediently, and then the nurse left them. Cassie was now utterly silent, staring hollow-eyed at her mother, waiting for answers. Lorna wrung her hands mutely, struggling for speech. Tears rolled down Lorna's face until Cassie was distraught. She leaned forward to clutch at both her mother's hands and pulling them towards her, desperate to know what had happened, but finding it impossible to ask. Finally her mother mouthed the words so quietly that Cassie could barely hear.

"Dad and Lizzie are in Intensive Care." Lorna paused and waited for Cassie to speak but Cassie said nothing; her face said it all. Taking a deep breath, the quiet whisper started again. "Dad's not too bad, but Lizzie's very poorly, Cass. Very poorly. In fact, they said she's...critical." Lorna's voice trailed off as it floundered on the terse medical judgement, her eyes focused firmly on the pillow next to her daughters' pale face, unable to look right at Cassie and meet the pleading expression. Mother and daughter stayed silent, struggling to accept the information, until Cassie lifted her head slightly from the pillow and opened her mouth to speak. As soon as she saw the movement, Lorna shuddered and began talking briskly and loudly, desperate to get away, before Cassie could ask the questions that her mother was trying *not* to think about.

"I've got to go back now, Cass. I have to see her before..."

"Let me come, mum," Cassie said quickly, sitting up in bed. "Let me come, I want to see her."

"No, love, its not nice, there are tubes everywhere."

"Please, mum." Cassie begged, fear gnawing at her intestines.

"When the tubes are off, Cass. Tomorrow, maybe."

"I want to see her now, mum. Please!"

"No, Cassie, it's no good. She wouldn't want you to see her like that. *I* can't bear to see it, so it would be too hard for you!" Lorna's voice rose in her distress.

"Mum, please. I have to see her!" Cassie sobbed hysterically, frightening Lorna, who stood up, panic-stricken. Cassie still clutched her mother's hands but Lorna pulled away from her daughter's grip, peeling off the fingers which fumbled and slid on the wet skin soaked with tears.

"I'm sorry, Cass." She whispered, as Cassie still clamoured, briefly glancing at her daughter's face, and wincing at what she saw there.

A nurse slid between the curtains like a shadow, drawn by the sound of the Cassie's sobbing. Lorna gave her a look of desperate entreaty, and the nurse answered with a sympathetic nod. Immediately, Lorna turned for one last anguished look at Cassie, and then pushed through the curtains with a wail of pain. Crying uncontrollably she ran clumsily and noisily from the ward. Cassie tried to leap out of bed after her, but the tubes of the drip clutched her arm possessively. Taking her by the shoulders, the nurse held Cassie gently but firmly against her chest, holding her while the sobs wracked her small body, allowing the child to exhaust herself with suffering. She knew there wasn't much chance of the sister surviving the night, and she felt desperately sorry for Lorna and Cassie. Finally, when the awful wailing had subsided into grizzling, she laid Cassie back on to the pile of pillows. Cassie allowed herself to be propped up, staring forward, but she didn't look at the nurse or even acknowledge her presence. The nurse was disappointed but undaunted. Removing the cap from a syringe, she added a sedative to the liquid in the tube of the drip. She checked Cassie's pulse and made a note on the chart at the end of the bed, before pushing the curtains back against the wall and chattering blandly in a strong Irish accent.

"Now then, we don't want you to be wandering about the place in the wee hours, so you do as your mammie says and see your sister tomorrow, it'll come soon enough. Now you're Cassandra and I'm Bridie so lets settle ourselves down together. I'll see about getting us a fresh pot of tea, what do you say to that?" Bridie smiled, as cheerfully as she could manage, then went off to the nurses' station to organise the beverage. She looked back at Cassie, but the girl turned away and glared obstinately at the bare walls. Bridie understood very well that Cassie was angry, and needed someone to vent her feelings on, she had seen it many times. She pottered about with the kettle and kept an eye on her young patient from a distance. Cassie laid in silence, still staring at the wall. The only object on the plain white plaster was a dark-ringed, grey-faced clock. Straining her eyes in the dull light she was able to watch dumbly as the hands moved slowly round. She was quiet now, but she fought for hours to stay awake.

It was just before dawn when her mother returned wearily to her bedside. The grey walls were at their most dismal when Lorna slumped down into the plastic chair at the side of the bed. Cassie swivelled hopefully towards her and stared, reading in her mother's face, the answer to the question she dare not ask. Lorna's look of despair frightened her into continued silence, she could not open her mouth. Lorna said nothing, she just sat, in a trance, gazing not at Cassie's face but at her white hospital pillow.

Cassie stared at her mother until night had turned to day. By then, the corner of the ward had become a softer, kinder, peach colour. Lorna's gaze faced blankly, emptily, forwards, and, all the time she was sitting there, Cassie was watching her.

It was if her mother had been petrified: nothing moved. Cassie was sure that her mother didn't even blink once. Lorna's eyes and mouth stayed open, in exactly the same position, the whole time Cassie was scrutinising her. The lips were slightly parted, as if to utter a feeble protest, but no word or sound came out, not even the faintest whisper of breathing.

Cassie was worried that her mother's eyes were drying out. The glassy surface of Lorna's lens had thickened, like an egg broken out of its shell will congeal and waste if left untended. The surfaces of the inner eyelids were so parched they were turning powdery and flaking away. It was as if her mother's face was cracking and falling apart from the eyes outward.

That was a terrifying thought – Cassie must stop it. Quickly, she raised her hand to pass it up and down in front of Lorna's face, in order to break her mother's line of vision, and make her look up, but Lorna gave no sign of noticing. Cassie kept repeating the gesture, becoming more and more frantic, but there was still no reaction, and then the nurses saw her and came over to check what was happening. One of them gently laid Cassie back onto her bed and smoothed the covers over her stiff, resisting body. It was the Irish nurse again; she bent and whispered to Cassie, her voice was soft, but utterly unyielding.

"Get some rest honey, try get some sleep. We will see to your Mamma, don't worry, she'll be alright." She promised, then both nurses bent to put their arms around Lorna's shoulders and lifted her to her feet. Lorna was clearly confused and stumbled as she walked away, unaware of where she was or what she was doing. She did not even remember to give Cassie a backward glance. Cassie was left alone in her bed, crying silently. She turned her back on the ward and faced the wall with its traitorous colour, hating the evidence that a new day had begun and that life was continuing, without Lizzie.

At that moment a cloud obscured the freshly risen sun and the wall was grey again. It gave Cassie, temporarily, a tiny portion of consolation. Soon after that, though, the nurses began their morning rounds, bringing drinks and medication to the sleepy patients, and the sun began to climb in earnest. Cassie could no longer deny the fact of time going on regardless. She turned to gaze at the clock again, now it seemed to swim before her eyes, taunting her, because of the tears that were brimming. She stared at it and wished hopelessly, begging in vain that the hands of the clock would go backwards instead of forwards.

Chapter 17

Nine months had passed since the accident, Cassie had told Talli, but what she hadn't said, was that it came back to haunt her every day in every detail. It was as if it had happened yesterday. The night drive had been the final treat of the short October holidays. Mum was upstairs, sorting out all the uniforms, when dad had returned home, eager to take the girls out for a drive in the new car.

"That car gets more attention than me!" Mum joked, as Mike gave it a final rubdown. Lizzie and Cassie had laughed as Mike lunged at Lorna with the duster, in retaliation. Cassie could see it all so clearly and she was glad. It was good that she could still remember everything. Well, not always good. She wished that she could forget some of the awful memories, especially when they seemed to want more attention than the nicer ones. She hoarded the happy times they had spent as a family. In the days and weeks after the accident, Cassie had struggled to amass multitudes of memories. Some part of every day was spent frantically recalling all the things her sister had ever said, religiously repeating jokes, silly stories, and every event she could think of. Sometimes she wondered if that was why she couldn't concentrate at school, because there were so many memories that must be maintained. Perhaps if she could write them all down carefully, she needn't worry about forgetting everything. She remembered what Talli had said, when she had talked about her secret, "Scribblemania", she had labelled it 'the cure for everything...'

After they got home from Oakwell, Cassie was sitting on her bedroom floor, alone and thoughtful. She'd been thinking about the accident, and the car journey today, and Savannah, and what Talli had said, and now something else had occurred to her. She was trying to recall what the lady at the Parsonage had told her, about Talli writing when she was older. Suddenly Cassie remembered: Talli had put her older sister, Maria, into the book, 'Jane Eyre.' She had written down her memories of her sister, and had hidden them in a story. Cassie rushed down stairs and went to find her mum, whirling into the kitchen excitedly and sending a mixing bowl flying. Luckily for Cassie and Lorna, the mixing bowl was waiting to be washed and did not contain anything.

"Mum, mum have we got Charlotte Brontë's book Jane Eyre?" Cassie demanded, picking up the bowl and placing it haphazardly on a pile of dishes in the sink.

"Hang on a minute! It's a good job that was empty." Lorna protested. She was tired, and still feeling vulnerable from the incident on the way home. "I'm in the middle of getting tea! I know you're really into the Brontës at the moment, but does it have to be right now? If you want to read something, have a look at that booklet I got from Oakwell, it's in a bag on the table. It mentions the sighting of a ghost at the Hall."

"Really?" Cassie's mouth went dry; she wasn't the only who had seen Talli then. Somehow she was disappointed; she'd wanted to think Talli had appeared just to her, though it was nice to know she wasn't dreaming.

"Who else has seen her?" she asked her mother.

"*Him*, actually Cass," Lorna replied, looking at her

daughter oddly, "William Batt, it says his name was. He was seen coming home to Oakwell, walking up the drive and into the house, at the exact same time as he was killed in London, I think in a fight or a battle, I'm not sure. Anyway, they said that he left a bloodstained footprint, which couldn't be cleaned off the wooden floors. In the end the wood itself had to be cut out because the mark disturbed some girls who were pupils at a school there. I told you Oakwell was a school in Charlotte Brontë's time, didn't I?" Cassie stared, transfixed by Lorna's words, remembering her vision of the soldier returning from battle, and the people in the dining room; she nodded vaguely to her mother but remained silent, lost in thought. She was no longer sure whether she had daydreamed at all. Lorna was pleased by Cassie's evident fascination, it made her feel that some small thing had gone right after all; she smiled at her daughter.

"It's a really good booklet, you ought to go and have a look at it."

"I will do, in a minute, but I want to look at Jane Eyre first." Cassie decided, breaking from her reverie and becoming fidgety. "You don't have to go and get it, just tell me where it is. Have we got the book?" Cassie continued anxiously, hopping from toe to toe in her enthusiasm. Lorna watched with amusement and relented.

"Well I admit it's nice to see you so interested in your schoolwork. Actually, I did that book at college so we *will* have a copy somewhere. Okay, okay, let me think." She paused for a moment, stirring a saucepan and frowning as she tried to remember, "Try the bookcase at the top of the stairs." She suggested finally, and smiled as Cassie whizzed off.

'Jane Eyre' was quickly found and Cassie took it into her room to sit on the floor; the bed had all sorts piled on it, the chair undiscoverable under a mountain of washing. She was happy on the floor, leaning on the bed. Turning the tattered cover revealed a sketch likeness of the author which gave Cassie a shock, the firm pencil lines delineated an older Charlotte Brontë with her pensive smile, but the face of the young 'Talli' was still easily recognisable. Cassie found it unnerving to find the familiar features hiding between the dusty pages. The lively eyes were averted, hiding their vivacity in shyness. It was a warm portrait and Cassie turned the pages with a wistful smile to begin reading the first chapter. She did not stop to think that she might have difficulty reading, though the print was small, the words seemed curiously familiar.

'There was no possibility of taking a walk that day.' The first line began innocently enough and Cassie was drawn up quickly into Charlotte's world.

Within minutes, Cassie was furiously indignant on behalf of the young heroine, Jane Eyre. Her heart went out to the ten-year-old orphan, who must be excluded from the cosy fireside of her rich relatives until she has "a more childlike disposition." Cassie's stomach lurched when she read of Jane's treatment at the hands of her cruel cousins. Name-calling and constant bullying were all too easy to empathise with; it was very similar to what she had to endure every day at school with Savannah. Cassie spirits revived when Jane finally retaliated, likening the main protagonist, her cousin John, to a murderer, a slave driver *and* a Roman Emperor. Bravely, Jane furiously fights his attack, and, even manages to hit him back! But the triumph was short-lived. Cassie's heart sinks when she reads of the appalling severity of Jane's punishment: her Aunt Reed sends her to be locked in the terrifying Red Room, the place where her late Uncle had died. As darkness falls, a strange light is seen. Jane sobs and screams in fear, but is thrust back into the dark room once again by her cruel guardian. The poor child collapsed into unconsciousness, just as Lorna called Cassie down for tea.

Cassie's parents were shocked to see their normally reticent daughter burning against the injustice of the wicked, fictional, aunt.

"It's only a story," Lorna ventured. "I'm sure it has a happy ending."

"It's not just a story, Mum. Charlotte Brontë's older sister is in that book, you know. Charlotte wrote about things that really happened, the lady at the Parsonage said so."

"Look, Cassie, I told you I read that book at college? Well, we had a lot of discussion about that bit, and you are partly right, Charlotte's older sister – Maria, was it? – is characterised as Helen Burns, but the rest is a story. The Brontës were really good at making up stories, so please don't upset yourself about Jane Eyre, or I'll have to speak to Mrs Harrison."

"No! Don't do that, don't do that, mum." Cassie begged, genuinely concerned. Lorna frowned, her tone became more gentle.

"You do get caught up in these stories, love, it's like that Titanic video, you got so emotional about that."

"Yes, but Lorna, even I know the Titanic was real!" Mike grinned and Lorna forced a smile.

"You know what I mean, that love story was entirely

made up, and the dancing scene, how realistic was that?" she asked, with such genuine confusion that they all laughed and Mike added jovially.

"There's nothing wrong with adding a little artistic licence; if it's good enough for Charlotte Brontë then it's good enough for us, eh, Cassie?"

"You're not helping, Mike," Lorna answered, pushing him half-heartedly. Mike smiled and patted his daughter's arm. She looked up from her meal and returned his smile absently, but her thoughts were already far off with the fictitious fortunes of Jane Eyre. She couldn't wait to go back and find out what happened next.

Chapter 18

When Cassie returned to the book she was relieved to find that, after the terrible scene in the Red Room, Jane Eyre was now comfortably ensconced in the safety of her own bed, being cared for by an apothecary. Cassie paused from the book to think what Mrs Harrison had said in class about the calling of the apothecary, or "doctor to the poor", instead of requesting a visit from a qualified physician.

"It's just as if you asked the local chemist to pop round and have a look at you. Everything had to be paid for then, visits from the doctor, medicines, bandages. We take the Health Service for granted, but people died because they couldn't afford to call the doctor!" The teacher looked round at the nonchalant children and raised her voice to continue.

"It might not be a thing of the past forever. You must have seen the recent leaflets and advertisement campaign that encourage you to 'Ask the Pharmacist'. That's just the start of it. If the Government starts to charge for doctors appointments, then by the time you all have children, we could be back in the 18th Century, so to speak!" She surveyed the class with a wry smile and patted her greying hair thoughtfully, before moving on. Something about the sardonic tone held Cassie's attention and even now she remembered the lesson perfectly; an expression of distaste crossed her face and she bent to her book, rapidly banishing thoughts of Mrs

Harrison. The apothecary in Talli's book was a kind man, who encouraged his young patient to talk to him. Cassie found it frustrating when Jane struggled to answer his questions, yet she, more than anyone, understood how difficult it was to talk about emotions.

Following the apothecary's visit, Jane waits and waits for change. Days, weeks, pass, while she becomes a Cinderella, following the orders of a servant. Finally, salvation arrives in the form of the dark figure of Mr Brocklehurst, described in the book as "A black pillar." 'Where have I heard that expression before?' Cassie wondered. Then, she remembered that someone had whispered it into her ear when she was at the Parsonage and about to be told off by Mrs Harrison. She had thought at the time that it was Savannah talking, but it was clearly a phrase that Talli knew; perhaps she had been hiding in one of the rooms just nearby, watching. Cassie smiled and carried on with the book.

Mr Brocklehurst interviews, (or rather interrogates, Cassie thought), Jane before agreeing to enrol her as a pupil at his school some fifty miles away.

Fifty miles didn't seem so far, Cassie pondered, an hour in the car, depending on the roads, *and who was driving*, she thought with a grimace; but Jane was placed alone into the noisy and uncomfortable horse-drawn coach at six in the morning, travelling through dismal January weather, on a day of 'preternatural length'. She finally arrives, long after dark, on a wild and windy night, at her new home, Lowood.

Cassie remained absorbed in Jane Eyre for the whole day on Sunday, and on Monday morning when she approached the school entrance, her thoughts still swam with the cruelties inflicted on the child. Leaning on the wall at one side of the school gate was Savannah; an acolyte casually looped around each arm. She was waiting for Cassie and stood up when she saw her, moving forward to bar her way when she walked through the gate. As soon as Cassie was within earshot, Savannah started her speech; the words ejected so savagely that spittle showered the air in front of her.

"Here she is. Cassandra Edwards, the daughter of a killer! He's already killed once, *his own daughter.*" Savannah pronounced with a smirk of satisfaction; she could see the tears well up instantly in Cassie's eyes; she was waiting for them to roll down her cheeks.

"I told you about Saturday when her father came after me, didn't I? The lunatic tried to kill me and dear, brave Prince. The poor thing was nervy all weekend, and daddy thinks one of his fetlocks may have been strained in all the panic." Cassie wasn't thinking straight, she stood silent as if she were in a trance, her body tensed with the pain. Her fists were clenching and unclenching automatically, she wasn't aware of them moving at all, but the words Savannah said were going into her like needles, every one of them.

"Mummy's just as upset. We've told the vet all about it and he said people like that should be reported!" Savannah looked at Poppy for sympathy and Poppy patted her arm, Savannah smiled at her and turned back to Cassie, this time her grin was wide across her face, and she licked her lips in anticipation before she pronounced her final sentence, loudly and clearly so that the whole playground could hear.

"*My* father said he will be ringing the police, because

the best thing to do with people like *her* father is lock them up and throw away the key!"

Without thinking, Cassie leapt at Savannah, her arms flying out in front of her, wildly trying to reach the corners of the smiling mouth. Astonished at the unexpected response, and trying to avoid Cassie's flailing hands, Savannah stepped back hastily, her movement pulling Poppy and Sophie back and off balance. Unfortunately, just behind them was a large kerbstone which jutted out, and Poppy fell heavily on to it. The injured party at once began yelling at full volume. The loud screams shocked Cassie out of her rage and she immediately dropped her hands to her sides. Her shoulders drooped, shrinking, in defeat. Savannah smiled and, ignoring her sobbing friend, calmly sent Sophie off to fetch the teacher on duty. Cassie's heart sank as she realised it was Mrs Harrison. When Mrs Harrison saw Cassie she gave her a furious look and scolded her angrily, having to raise her voice over the sound of Poppy's raucous shouts, in order to make herself heard.

"I might have known you would be behind this Cassandra. Now you're becoming a problem in the playground as well as in the classroom! We shall see what the Head has to say about this!"

Cassie stood watching, in silence, as Savannah made a pretence of soothing her friend, by patting her shoulder. The action was entirely for Mrs Harrison's benefit but Poppy seemed grateful and her crying subsided. This made it possible that Savannah could begin her complaints, and she promptly began wailing that Cassie had run at them for *no reason* and she, Savannah, was worried that poor dear Poppy had probably broken her back. At this, even Mrs Harrison's gullibility was over-stretched and she gestured impatiently that she wanted silence. Savannah crouched nobly by her friend, intermittently tossing back her long blonde hair and patting Poppy's hand, occasionally raising her other hand to wipe away an imaginary tear, and all the time whimpering sympathetically. Only when the teacher's attention was drawn away, did she dare exude glares of pure malice in Cassie's direction. After a brief examination, Poppy's condition was judged sufficiently satisfactory to enable her to be removed to the Head teacher's Office. Mrs Harrison indicated that Cassie should follow, and then Savannah began such a loud and vehement clamour of insistence that she, too, should accompany them, that Mrs Harrison's look of fury to her *almost* equalled the one which was given to Cassie herself. Savannah completely ignored the warning, and gained her point. She joined the others, and leading them triumphant through the crowd of children who had gathered, parted the numbers majestically with a wave, thoroughly enjoying the theatrics of portraying herself as a mini Moses. Mrs Harrison followed, trying to support a drooping Poppy, who basked in the unaccustomed attention. Cassie brought up the rear, idly thinking again of the young Jane Eyre, punished for striking back at the rich young tyrant who tormented her. In the book, Jane describes her actions as 'frantic' and says '*I don't very well know what I did with my hands*'. Cassie could have used exactly the same words herself, their situations were uncannily similar. When Jane's bully, cousin John, falls to the floor, he too '*bellowed out aloud.*' For him also, '*aid was near*'; his sisters had run for Mrs Reed. Cassie felt that it was typical of Savannah that she herself hadn't fallen, and instead Poppy had borne the brunt of Cassie's anger. There wasn't even a mark from Cassie's fingers on Savannah's face. 'I must have missed her,' Cassie thought, with guilty disappointment.

Jane had been sent to the Red Room and Cassie was being taken to the Head's Room. The comparison of their circumstances diverted Cassie slightly, reducing the terror, that she would otherwise have felt, on approaching the office of the Head Teacher. Indeed, something of Jane's rage burned against the injustice of walking through the assembled hordes like a criminal. Savannah's words wrenched her, their cruelty in talking of her father as a killer, when the inquest had *proven* it was the lorry driver who had lost control of his vehicle. The man had been adjusting his radio, the technical difficulties experienced by the radio station that night had been cited, as part of a 'tragic string of events', in the local headlines for a few days. People had debated the use of entertainment in transport through the letters page. All eyes had been on Cassie every day at school as her sister's photograph had appeared in each evening's paper. Lizzie was very photogenic, and so any letter that appeared to relate to the discussion, however obliquely, had been printed with the photo adjoining it and a succinct caption. 'Local girl Elizabeth Edwards who was tragically killed when a radio station went off the air'. The lorry was rarely mentioned in these brief notices for fear of litigation by the driver, so that people had begun to think it was the car driver who had been at fault. When her father tried to return to work in a busy sales environment it was gently suggested that a more suitable, less stressful, position would be available in the administration department, away from the public gaze. Suddenly Mike found that his former colleagues avoided his company; he felt it as an accusation. He tried to speak out but the wheelchair detracted from his previous aura of authority and nobody listened to his extensive explanations. In desperation, he too had written to the newspaper but his words had not been published as the letter merely related *the truth* of the events leading to his daughter's death. The Editor concluded that as all this information had been printed at the time of the inquest, further repetition would hold no interest to the readers. A blank acknowledgement slip had been the only communication from the newspaper, the receipt of which flung her father into a long period of withdrawal. He felt utterly unable to return to work and accepted the package they offered him to leave. The debate about radios and cars continued throughout the letters pages for some weeks afterward, each letter still accompanied by the photograph of Lizzie, but her father no longer attempted to set the record straight. Instead he asked Lorna to purchase a national paper, one which did not carry regional news, and these days Mike sat at the table apparently absorbed in the antics of self-appointed celebrities and minor royalty. Cassie knew that Savannah's father considered himself a local notary and searched each edition of the evening paper for references to himself of pictures of his only child . Savannah was always bragging about her own and her father's appearance in the 'local rag' as she called it. Copies were brought to show in class, every time her father's name, or a picture of Savannah on her pony was printed; the extra issues were distributed thoughtfully to chosen classmates. Interestingly, despite the family's obvious wealth, there were never *quite* enough newspapers to go round each of the children who professed friendship, so that a careful selection process by Savannah was necessary to determine which friend should receive the prize. The more Cassie thought about it, the more she realised that there was no doubt in her mind as to where Savannah had received her information from.

Chapter 19

The Head Teacher's office was at the very back of the school, hidden in a maze of unfamiliar corridors. It seemed hours before they arrived. Mrs Harrison gestured Cassie and Savannah to sit outside as she went in to the office first, her arm beginning to be impatient in its position about the shoulders of the still whining Poppy. Even Savannah was subdued by their proximity to authority and remained silent, contenting herself with directing sly kicks at Cassie's ankles as she swung her legs, aiming to appear nonchalant should any one pass. Cassie winced once as Savannah's heavy heeled shoes caught her shin, but otherwise remained unmoved. Outwardly she sat obediently, if somewhat blankly, facing forward. Inwardly she was oblivious to her surroundings, in her mind's eye she was far, far away. Absorbed in a daydream, she had become the diminutive Jane, stepping across her Aunt's room to meet the terrifying figure of Mr Brocklehurst.

"And are you a good child?" boomed a harsh voice, looming down, to Jane Eyre.

"Are you daydreaming again, child?" came another, more abrasive voice, rather vehemently into Cassie's ear, "Cassandra Edwards!" The tone changed briefly, became deferential, "Really, Mr Miller you see what I have to put up with," then the full force of the anger was back again: "MISS EDWARDS!"

"Yes, Mrs Harrison, thank you. Perhaps you had

better get along to the rest of the class. I will wait with Poppy until her parents arrive and you can take Savannah back with you. We don't want her to miss any of her valuable lesson time, do we?" Mr Miller instructed, his tone firm and his expression non-committal.

"No, Mr Miller. Thank you. Come along Savannah, dear, let's get you back. *I'll see you later*, Cassandra Edwards," Mrs Harrison promised warningly. Cassie nodded dumbly and allowed herself to be led into the Head Teacher's office. Once in, Mr Miller quietly closed the outside door, and then went across to the adjoining secretary's office.

"Mrs Bowles, I'll just close this door slightly while I speak to Cassandra. Don't want to disturb our patient, do we, Poppy? Call me when the parents get here, Mrs Bowles, I would like to have a word with them."

"Yes, Mr Miller," the secretary answered, and then the door was pulled partly closed, so that Cassie could still hear the quiet murmur of Mrs Bowles reassuring Poppy and sorting post at the same time. Mr Miller pointed to the chair opposite his desk.

"Have a seat, Cassandra," he said mildly, his face still remained non-judgemental, but his eyes burned into her as if he were reading her thoughts. He paused for a moment as he stared while he considered something, then, satisfied, resumed.

"Now then, Miss Edwards. What's all this about?" Instantly tears welled in Cassie's eyes and her throat contracted; she felt she was nearly choking on the words she was unable to speak. Mr Miller observed her distress and spoke kindly.

"Take your time Cassandra," he suggested. He was

about to continue when he was interrupted by the voice of Mrs Bowles calling through from her office.

"Mr Miller, sir, I can see the parents coming across the car park. Are you coming through?"

"Yes, Mrs Bowles. Wait here, will you Cassandra? I'll be back in a minute." Exiting his office, Mr Miller carefully closed the door behind him and Cassie was left alone with her thoughts. Mr Miller did not seem so terrifying as she had expected, the gentle manner in which he had spoken to her confused her. Again her thoughts turned back to the story of Jane Eyre, but this time to the rather happier encounter of Jane with the apothecary, who had visited her during her illness. Cassie had been struck by Talli's words in the book, "*Children can feel, but they cannot analyse their feelings,*" and now she felt again how true they were. While she had been thinking, her gaze had wandered idly about the office, without Cassie taking much notice of what information her eyes were relaying to her brain, but suddenly her senses were alert, something had caught her attention. She sprang up and walked across the room, impelled by some inner prompting. She stopped by the wall next to the window and her heart leapt as she recognised the small sketch displayed in the frame in front of her. It was the same she had surveyed in her book at home, the pencil drawing of Charlotte Brontë. Seeing the picture prompted her to remember more of Jane Eyre, especially the awful description of life at Lowood, which Charlotte Brontë had based on her own experiences. The conditions the girls were expected to live in were harsh by any standards; freezing bedrooms so bitterly cold that the water in the wash basin was solid, "nauseous" burnt porridge for breakfast, rancid meat for dinners. The children were forced to struggle to church across the snowy hills without boots, the snow got into their shoes and melted there. Cassie winced at the thought; surrounded by double-glazing and central heating she found it hard to imagine such discomforts. Reading about Helen Burns, however, made the hairs on the back of her neck stand on end: *everything about her sounded familiar.* Jane Eyre's thoughts about Helen, standing in the middle of the schoolroom, made Cassie's heart beat slow. "*She looks as if she were thinking of something beyond her punishment – beyond her situation: of something not round her nor before her....Her eyes are fixed on the floor but I am sure they do not see it. Is she in a day dream now?*" Laura's words to Cassie on the coach echoed Talli's written ones exactly. Reading on, Cassie had been astonished to see Mrs Harrison's own descriptions on the page before her. "*Hardened girl,*" Miss Scratcherd says to Helen Burns, "*Nothing can cure you of your slatternly habits.*" Mrs Harrison had used the same words in one of Cassie's after school lectures. Cassie remembered now that it was when the class had already begun studying the Brontës, and Mrs Harrison must have picked up the phrases when making the notes for the lessons, but even so the similarities were disturbing, and made Cassie shudder to think of, especially as Helen had just been beaten on the neck with a bundle of sticks. Standing in the headmasters office, looking at Talli's picture and remembering, Cassie's hand went involuntarily to her own neck and clutched it protectively.

Only Miss Temple would have provided some consolation for life at Lowood. Described by Helen as "full of goodness," Miss Temple is the teacher that releases the true power of Helen's mind. By praising her liberally and encouraging her in her interests, Helen comes alive. The book describes her cheeks glowing and eyes shining, as she expands on subjects as diverse as ancient history and scientific advancements, a complete contrast to the disorganised day dreamer failing in class.

Miss Temple becomes the first adult that Jane can finally open up to; carefully following Miss Temple's instructions to "add nothing and exaggerate nothing", Jane recounts her sad history. Miss Temple is then able to clear Jane's name, after she is publicly accused of being a liar by Mr Brocklehurst; Jane is able to make a fresh start; and things start to improve.

Cassie smiled to remember as she looked at Talli's picture, half-heartedly searching the face for some message. The eyes remained averted, but Cassie thought she could read pain now in the slight frown across the forehead, and impatient disapproval in the firm set of the mouth. She was puzzled at first but then a chill went down her spine as she realised she had indeed forgotten something.

Helen Burns was only a fictional character, but Cassie already knew that much of what was written about her was true. Helen was based on Maria Brontë, Talli's elder sister, who had suffered at school and become so ill that she had been sent home to die.

"I'm sorry." Cassie murmured to the picture and her eyes filled with tears, blurring her vision, so that it seemed, momentarily, as if the printed lines of Talli's features glanced sympathetically in her direction, before resuming her original position.

Cassie was still standing by the wall, gaining solace

from the familiar outlines, when Mr Miller re-entered the room. He seemed surprised to find her out of her chair, but came over to stand beside her. Looking at the portrait, he smiled benignly.

"Know who it is?"

"Oh, yes," Cassie replied enthusiastically. "My friend Talli, er, I mean, Charlotte Brontë."

"Your friend?" Mr Miller queried, but then answered himself. "Oh, of course, you've been learning all about the Brontës. Your class went to the Parsonage at Howarth; am I right?"

"Yes, it was wonderful. To meet Charlotte was so amazing," Cassie continued warmly, but then suddenly stopped, realising she must sound foolish.

"Meet her? Oh of course," Mr Miller nodded. "I believe Mrs Harrison mentioned that the Parsonage had people dressed up as the family mingling around it, in order to give a real feel for the history. It obviously worked with you then, Cassandra. Hmm. I'll get the secretary to drop them a line, tell them how much impact it had. Very impressive." He turned and bent to rummage in his desk for notepad and paper, until Cassie began to feel she was quite forgotten.

"I'll go then, Mr Miller," she mumbled, heading for the door. Mr Miller looked up from his task, his face firm again.

"Just a moment, Cassandra. I am not unmindful as to the reason you are here. I want you to sit down and give me your version of events from this morning. Is that alright?" Cassie nodded and returned to her chair, gloomily. Once again she felt her throat contract and her chest tighten; she began to worry that she would find it impossible to speak, until she remembered how Jane

Eyre had been instructed to talk to Miss Temple: '*add nothing and exaggerate nothing*'. Cassie decided to do exactly the same. Slowly, she began to explain to Mr Miller what had happened, narrating only the precise words used by Savannah, and then carefully detailing the effects of the newspaper coverage on her family. Mr Miller listened silently, his face grave. When she had finished, he spoke briefly.

"Cassandra, what you have told me has obviously been a problem for some time. I'm glad you were able to confide in me, and I want to be honest with you. I think you and your parents may need to talk about this with someone who will be able to help you more than I can, someone who is qualified in dealing with such matters. It's something called counselling. I'm sure you'll have heard of it before?" He raised his eyebrows in query and Cassie nodded. She had heard of counselling only once, her dad had been offered it and had refused, rather rudely. Luckily, Mr Miller did not stop to ask her what she had heard, he just carried on.

"I'll have to contact your parents, of course, but I don't want you to feel that my talking to them is a punishment. Don't worry, will you?" he asked, noticing the look of panic sweep across Cassie's face. "As for this morning's incident, I will speak to all concerned and make sure that everyone is aware of the situation. I will get Savannah on her own and we'll see what she says then, but if she ever does anything like that again, come and tell me. Don't knock her down, otherwise I will have to reprimand *you*. Now, does all that sound alright?" Cassie nodded and managed a small smile. She felt quite shocked, she had expected a terrible reaction, yet the hard faced Head Teacher she had always feared, was looking at her now with genuine concern in his shrewd eyes. It was not like the anger she had to deal with from...

"Mrs Harrison!" Cassie burst out, guiltily flinching.

"What about Mrs Harrison?" Mr Miller enquired gently.

"She might not like it, sir. She might think I, I'm getting away with it," Cassie said quickly, her face flaming.

"Don't worry, we'll get the educational psychologist to have a word. She has a wonderful way of dealing with difficult behaviour."

"Difficult behaviour, Mr Miller, is that me?" Cassie asked slowly. Mr Miller allowed himself a half-smile. "Not *just* you. She's very positive, I think you'll get on just fine. Her name is Miss Temple."

"Miss Temple?" Cassie repeated, astonished.

"Do you know her?" Mr Miller seemed surprised.

"Her name is familiar, Sir," Cassie said, smiling genuinely now, and with a new air of confidence, which made her quite a different child, Mr Miller observed.

"Come along then, I'll take you back to your classroom. I'll have a word with Mrs Harrison while I'm there."

Cassie followed Mr Miller along the empty corridors. The classrooms were now full with the industrious murmur of children quietly working, or the lone, clear voice of a teacher.

"This Literacy Hour really works well," Mr Miller commented, as much to himself as Cassie. "It reminds me of the teaching I learnt in college. Ah, here we are, your classroom. Just in time, I think Mrs Harrison is ready to begin." Mr Miller opened the door and gently waved Cassie through, "Mrs Harrison, could I just have a moment please before you start?" Mrs Harrison came quickly across to the doorway, gloating with her triumph, and evidently eager to hear of Cassie's retribution for her crime. Mr Miller led her out into the corridor and shut the door firmly, so that nothing of their conversation could be heard. Cassie moved slowly between the desks towards her seat, keeping her head down. Savannah was whispering furiously to the girl sitting next to her, their eyes gleamed, glued to Cassie's face, searching for signs of weakness. The rest of the class watched silently, focusing firstly on Cassie, then to Savannah, then on the closed classroom door; eyes swivelling like those of spectators tracking the ball at a tennis match. Only Laura reached across and put her hand on Cassie's arm. Cassie looked up and Laura smiled tentatively, she was about to speak when a loud bang frightened her into silence. The door into the classroom had been pushed roughly open and Mrs Harrison entered, evidently displeased. The class instantly sprang to attention and faced forward. Savannah gave one last, threatening, glare at Cassie before turning round. Mrs Harrison crossed straight to her desk and picked up her notes to begin the lesson. She did not look in Cassie's direction once.

Chapter 20

Towards the end of that week, Cassie was sitting at her desk, daydreaming as usual, when her attention was caught by Mrs Harrison's sudden mention of the Brontës. The Literacy Hour was just coming to a close and the teacher was giving out their homework.

"...and as we have been studying the Brontës, I have decided on a rather ambitious project. Because Monday is staff training day, you have before you a lovely, long weekend. I don't want you to waste all that extra time, so..." She paused, trying to gauge their reaction, then announced triumphantly, "you are going to follow the Brontës' fine example and make your own books!"

The class were silent; not one of them exhibited any sign of enthusiasm whatsoever. Mrs Harrison was disappointed. After a moment, Brian called out.

"Oh, yeah, do we get them pens we had last week, Miss?" Mrs Harrison glared at him causing Jason to snort into his sleeve.

"No, we are not repeating the feather and ink fiasco we had on Friday, nor do I expect you to spend all Saturday sewing sugar bags into book covers, although I'm sure some of you would prefer that to actually *writing* in them. You are very fortunate in that I have spent many hours stapling paper pages into cardboard covers. I only require you to fill those pages." At this a groan went up from the class, especially Jason's crowd. Brian was looking over at them eagerly; he tried to impress the others, by giving a snort of displeasure that was of elephantine proportions; Jason nodded approval and Brian was satisfied. Mrs Harrison gave Brian a look of disgust and continued.

"Now, adopting the Brontës as a model does not mean that you have to write a full length novel. That would be wonderful, if not a miracle!" The teacher enjoyed an amused smile at the impossibility of the thought, then resumed her address.

"Branwell and Charlotte both created magazines as children, with a variety of different writing included; plays, poems, prose which was written by the Brontës under the guise of other persona, letters and even their own advertisements some of which are quite humorous. From this wide selection you will be... yes, Savannah?" Mrs Harrison stopped to acknowledge the arm waving impertinently, diverting the attention of the class.

"Miss, what's a persona?"

"Good question, dear, I'm pleased you were paying such close attention. A persona is a character that the author assumes in their writing. Some would say it is a way of masking your own innermost feelings. The Brontë children used a few, they were four great genii, sometimes, in their early 'Young Men' plays and then Charlotte Brontë often wrote using the persona of her hero, the Duke of Wellington, when she was your age. You could write stories as if *you* were your hero, Savannah, who would that be?"

"Me, miss, you mean who do I fancy? Oooh, let me think."

"No, dear. Who would you most like to emulate?" Savannah looked blank, Mrs Harrison tried a different approach,

"Savannah, who is the person whose characteristics you most admire?"

"Oooh Miss, I don't admire anyone's characteristics, who said I did?" Savannah said, her voice quivering in a tone of utmost innocence, but with such an expression of mischief on her face, that Mrs Harrison could not possibly be fooled any longer.

Mrs Harrison looked down at her desk in utter exasperation, Savannah was sniggering with her friends, triumphant that she had reduced the teacher to silence. Eventually Mrs Harrison looked up, evidently still disconcerted, and raising her eyes she looked right at Cassie, who was, for once, facing forward attentively, clearly eager to hear more. For one moment their eyes locked together, then Mrs Harrison pulled her attention back to the books she had on the desk in front of her. Once again, she continued her instructions to the class, but this time her voice had lost its customary power and was instead hesitant and placatory.

"As I was saying, you have a very wide selection of different writing styles to choose from. I'm sure you will all be able to produce something, even the daydreamers among us, Cassandra Edwards, though I'm pleased to note that you have been paying attention just now, well done." With that, Mrs Harrison glanced briefly in Cassie's direction, her eyes wary, almost admitting an apology, before picking up the pile of little books so carefully made and distributing them round the class. When Cassie received hers, she was delighted to find that her book was enclosed in bright yellow card. The cheerful exuberance of the colour instantly brought to mind the sunny group she had seen, quietly working in Oakwell Hall; and that gave her an idea. Instantly, she picked up her pencil and wrote in large, slightly spidery writing on the front cover the title of her story.

★ ★ ★

Cassie left school that afternoon enthusiastically clutching her yellow book. She rushed quickly home, her mind overflowing with ideas and conversations, which she would put onto the pages. She knew *now* why Talli had changed so much when she spoke of Scribblemania! She felt alive! Words were whispering into her brain, her fingers fidgeted, with pulses of prose eager to be written down. Crossing the busy road near her house, she barely stopped for the traffic, she was so engrossed in her imaginary world. She skipped up the path and flung the door open, dumping her bag at one side and only just remembering to take off her shoes.

"Hello, I'm home!" Cassie called out and ran happily through to the kitchen, to tell her parents all about her book. She was met by an empty silence.

"Mum, Dad!!" she shouted excitedly, searching for them.

"We're in here, Cassandra." The toneless voice of her father came from the front room. Cassie stopped in her tracks, surprised; they never used that room except for guests, and she didn't know they were expecting any one.

"Come in here, love, please." Her mother asked, the voice quiet but firm. Still puzzled, Cassie paused in the doorway. She was struck, anew, by the dismal coldness of the dark blue walls. Her parents had been going to decorate this room, when the October half term ended last year and the two girls had gone back to school. Beautiful, bright yellow floral wallpaper that Lorna and her daughters had chosen together was piled up in the pantry. Cassie remembered bringing it home as if it had been yesterday. Her dad had complained it was far too girlie for him. He protested that he would never be able to sit in there once the 'funky flowers' were everywhere, but they had all laughed. Lizzie had asked if she could help her dad put the border on. Mike had smiled, put his arms round her and said "what would I do without my right hand man?" hugging his daughter proudly. That had been two days before the accident. Entering the room now, full of thoughts of her sister, Cassie went to sit silently on a lone chair in the corner. Her father sat huddled at one end of the settee, a place he usually avoided because of the difficulty he had in getting up again; his empty wheelchair was waiting, on the carpet next to him, perched like an expectant vulture. Its presence was irritating, irrefutable proof of Mike's lessened ability. Her mother was curled up, foetal-style, in the other chair, in the far corner. The room was chilly, despite the fact that it was a sunny day and Cassie shivered involuntary. Her father noticed the movement and frowned in distaste, he was silent for a moment but then forced himself to speak.

"We had a visitor today." He announced, looking at Cassie steadily.

"Oh," Cassie murmured, staring with confusion at her father's expression, trying to read it in the shadowy dimness. The light in here was very poor, heavy curtains and thick nets prevented the sunshine from entering. They had been there when Mike and Lorna bought the house, and would have been replaced, as part of the redecoration.

"Who was it?" She asked tentatively. Mike had been

waiting for the question.

"You should know!" he barked. Cassie jumped nervously, tears pricked at her eyes. She desperately tried to think what had happened then realisation dawned and she felt sick to the pit of her stomach.

"Mike!" Lorna intervened, sliding up into a sitting position. "Don't be so hard on her, you know what Mr Miller said." She looked across at Cassie sympathetically.

"Yes. I know. She's twisted him round her little finger with all those sob stories. Face it, Lorna, she attacked another child."

"She was defending you," Lorna replied, cautiously.

"From what? *Words I never would have known about.*" Mike shouted angrily at Lorna, then turned to Cassie, "You've no business sending people round here pitying me! I'm alive!" He observed bitterly. "It's yourself you should pity, turning the water works on and saying all those things to get you out of trouble. Your head is in the clouds, that's your problem. You're no use to anyone in the real world!" With that, he launched himself violently upwards, one arm holding on to the corner of the settee, the other flailing at the air. He was faltering, unbalanced; he grabbed precariously at the edge of the mantelpiece as he tried to aim himself at the wheelchair. Lorna leapt up to help him, and he, reluctantly, accepted her assistance to get into the seat. Once he was sitting down he forced the wheels down furiously and pushed himself out of the room. Lorna was compelled to follow after him. Cassie remained crouched in the chair in the dismal room, crying bitterly. From the distant dining room she could hear her fathers angry bursts interspersed with her mothers sobs and desperate entreaties. Cassie remained there for some time, paralysed by grief, before finally creeping quietly to her room and staying there.

Later, Lorna brought her some sandwiches and sat down on the end of Cassie's bed. She said nothing at all. It was not that she *wanted* to sit on her daughter's bed in absolute, awful silence, just that Lorna had utterly no idea what to say. Her eyes were red and swollen and her throat was sore from crying. She didn't really want Cassie to see her like this, anyway. Cassie had buried herself in the pillows, trying to stifle her tears. She could not bring herself to sit up or even turn round; she kept her face hidden and didn't respond to her mother; though she was acutely aware of her presence. After sitting with her daughter, in silence, for fifteen minutes Lorna could stand it no longer and went downstairs. Only then did Cassie lift her head up from the damp pillow, but it was too late; her mother had already gone and she didn't go back to Cassie's room again.

Chapter 21

Cassie awoke the next day still wearing her crumpled school clothes, having fallen asleep on top of her quilt. The room was bright and the sunlight that streamed in through the thin curtains was scattering patterns on the pale wallpaper. It reminded Cassie of the sea. She was mesmerised by the moving colours, her eyes drawn into following the blue-green patches, which surged backwards and forwards, like the tide, every time a slight breeze rippled the fabric of the curtain.

The patterns made her think of Laura. Laura had gone to the coast this weekend, in fact, she would be there now, Cassie realised. Since the school trip to Howarth, Laura and Cassie had spent every break time walking round the playground together. At first they talked casually, discussing television programmes, magazines, and music; then gradually they drifted towards school related topics, an incident in a different class, an allusion to another teacher, but never discussing Mrs Harrison. Families had been out of bounds too, until yesterday. The sudden mention of a visit, to Laura's grandmother at the coast, was the first time Cassie had heard anything of Laura's relatives.

"We're going tonight. Dad hates rushing over one day, and back the next, so he's taken the day off and we'll be stopping till Monday. I'll bring you some rock back, shall I?" she suggested timidly. Cassie smiled weakly in response, unable to tell Laura that she never ate rock, and burning with curiosity to hear more about Laura's previously unknown family.

"Is it just you and your dad? Who else is going?" she burst out, regretting it immediately as Laura visibly blanched. The harmless question threw Laura into a panic. She'd always avoided mentioning families because she knew all about Lizzie now, everyone did. Savannah had made sure the whole school knew of the reason why Cassie had escaped punishment for hurting Poppy. Savannah had been extremely careful to avoid talking to Cassie herself or give any appearance of going near her at all. By carefully following Cassie at a safe distance and then, if Cassie appeared to be moving in Savannah's direction, quickly swirling round with her nose in the air, Savannah encouraged the others to avoid Cassie totally.

"Don't get too near!" she would hiss loudly, if any one seemed to be approaching Cassie. "Even if she does something to you, it's not her that could be in trouble, it's you."

The warnings were on the whole unnecessary. Most people kept out of Cassie's way anyway, because after hearing all about Lizzie, they had no idea what to say.

Laura was the only one who had been able to talk to Cassie, relatively freely, until now at any rate. The pause before Laura's reply lengthened into awkwardness and Cassie shifted uncomfortably, furious with herself. Why had she asked Laura such a personal question?

"We're all going, all the family," Laura finally replied, rapidly changing the subject. "What are you doing this weekend, Cass?" There was a long exhalation of breath as Cassie let out a disappointed sigh.

"Nothing. I though perhaps we could have met up somewhere." She said it on the spur of the moment;

knowing that Laura would be away, but as she lay in her bed on the Saturday morning, she wished it had been possible. The weekend stretched before her, blank and challenging, the extra day off school taunting her. Normally she'd have jumped at the chance of a day at home, away from Mrs Harrison. Any excuse would have sufficed; dentist, stomach ache, the slightest chance of a cold, but now the atmosphere in the house was tangible. Mike and Lorna had made no further plans for trips out, after the disaster of the previous Saturday, and, after last night's reception, Cassie certainly didn't think there would be any enthusiasm for spontaneous excursions, even if she *could* think of somewhere suitable for the wheelchair. She got up wearily and changed out of her school clothes. Washing her face in the bathroom, she heard the murmur of her parent's voices downstairs. Cassie hurried down hopefully, but, when she walked into the kitchen, it was to meet with a grim silence. Her father was sat at the table forcing his model kit into shape with tight-lipped determination, busily battening down the matches and snapping any miscreants with ruthless satisfaction. Lorna was emptying the kitchen cupboards, stacking tins into towers, ignoring the ones that fell off the pile and landed on the floor with a damaging thud. She thrust a cloth furiously behind the doors, rubbing madly and muttering about mess. Cassie watched the tensed shoulders and jolting motion for a few long seconds, before greeting her mother's back, in a brave attempt at cheerfulness.

"Hi, mum, do you want a hand?" The vigorous movements stopped but Lorna didn't turn round, instead a faded black sweater addressed her daughter briskly.

"Haven't you got any homework?"

"Well, yes," Cassie admitted. "But I'd prefer to help you. You'd be finished quicker then."

"Don't worry about me, Cass, I don't need any assistance. Homework is far more important."

"You're not trying to get out of it, are you?" Mike muttered from the table, his head still bent over his model. Cassie turned to look at him. His hair looked greyer than she remembered. She realised with a shock that he had aged suddenly; almost all the rich black hair he had been so fond of had been replaced. She couldn't understand how he had let this happen, he had always been so careful with his appearance. Lorna and Lizzie had enjoyed teasing him whenever a new grey hair had appeared. The disgust on his face had made them laugh and then the performance of plucking out each offending strand had caused them to taunt him mercilessly. Mike would stand in front of the mirror, alternately ranting at his family, and the hairs, until each individual grey was removed, and only the black remained.

"Thick hair for a man," he'd say vainly, studying his reflection and quoting the polite, solitary praise of a trainee hairdresser, long ago. The oft repeated phrase would send them all into streams of sarcastic commentary, that was soon followed by more laughter. Now, though, Mike's hair was definitely much thinner and the grey hairs totally outnumbered the black ones; her dad would be bald if he pulled them all out.

"Are you going to get that homework done then?" Lorna called from behind the cupboard door.

"Yes, we don't want another visit from school." Mike added grumpily. Cassie made no reply. She watched them both sadly, each buried in their task. Neither turned to offer an encouraging smile, but she stood there, waiting, just in case. She picked up one of her dad's matches and rolled it, up and down, up and down between her fingers, half-hoping they would tell her off for wasting time. After a few minutes silent vigil, in which it became clear to her that nothing was going to change, she carefully replaced the match on the table, and wandered back to her bedroom. It was only after he heard her feet going slowly, miserably, up the stairs, that her father looked up from his matchsticks. He stared at the place where Cassie had been standing, not more than an arm's length away, and something inside collapsed. He stretched out his hand to the place where Cassie's fingers had touched the table, and lifted the small match she had been playing with. He gazed at the tiny, fragile, piece of wood, so easily broken, and he knew he had failed again. Then he closed his hand around the match and clutched it to his chest, while his eyes streamed with silent tears.

Chapter 22

The first sentence was the hardest, she had no idea how to start it. She knew, of course, that 'once upon a time' was out of the question, Mrs Harrison would laugh heartily at that, she'd probably read it out. Cassie sat on the end of her bed, flicking through her magazines, hoping, in vain, that one of them would suggest a suitable opening line. She pulled off some of her and Lizzie's Jacqueline Wilson books from the bookcase and looked at the first lines, "*My name is Tracy Beaker*". Good for Jacqueline Wilson, she was famous, but no good for Cassie's homework, she could hardly write "*My name is Cassandra Edwards*", Mrs Harrison would accuse her of a lack of imagination. She tried another of the Jacqueline Wilson favourites, 'The Suitcase Kid': "*When my parents split up they didn't know what to do with me.*" That sounded better, she could put "*when my sister died, my parents didn't know what to do with me.*" It was true, but... too painful. It would look like she was begging for sympathy. After going through the rest of the book case, and leaving its contents scattered all over the bedroom floor, she finally turned to the beginning of Jane Eyre in the search for inspiration.

"*There was no possibility of taking a walk that day.*" It hardly seemed earth shattering. Mrs Harrison always told the class to ask of the opening sentence:

"How does it set the scene, what does it tell you about the character?" It seemed to Cassie that Charlotte's first line merely pointed out that it was a bad day for walking! But knowing what happened to poor Jane, later that same day, when the bored, unexercised cousins search for her, looking for entertainment, it *could* suggest that all circumstances, even the weather, were conspiring against her. Cassie thought about her sister's death, the slippy roads, the radio station going off the air, the chance meeting on a country lane. A freak accident, the inquest had said. She decided to adapt Talli's beginning; it seemed to fit Lizzie's life. Grabbing a piece of scrap paper, she began scribbling furiously.

"*There was a good chance they would be able to go out for a drive that evening, after all. The rain had stopped in the afternoon, and a watery sunshine was half-heartedly drying the pavements. The two girls were looking eagerly out of their bedroom window, waiting for their father to return in the new car.*

"*The roads will still be slippy,*" *Lizzie commented.* "*But dad's such a good driver, it won't matter." Cassandra looked up at her older sister and nodded in agreement. She never questioned her sibling's authority, nor did their parents. Lizzie never told lies or exaggerated, so Mike and Lorna trusted implicitly every word she said.*"

Abruptly, Cassie stopped writing; she wondered whether she should change their names, she could pretend it was a story. Her father's words stung her ears, 'saying these things to get you out of trouble.' He would be furious if she wrote about Lizzie. She wondered how Talli's father had reacted to her stories, and then she remembered that the young Brontës had written their compositions in tiny writing, barely discernible to the human eye. They had had to use the magnifying glass to read them. Cassie was struck by a sudden vision of a small brown hand, stretching out over hers, to grab the magnifying glass at the Brontë Parsonage. They had kept their stories a secret; perhaps she could do the same. She could try and write it really small, it would be hard, because putting her pen to the paper and concentrating didn't guarantee results. Many a time, she had watched in horror, as the spidery scrawl set off by itself across the page, and she seemed helpless to stop it. Just the thought of the struggle ahead was enough to make her give up, and she got up and left her room. Halfway down the stairs, she paused, the mute atmosphere emanated from the rooms below. She could hear the quiet noise of her parents moving, the click of the matches, the banging of the cupboard doors, but neither of them spoke. From outside, her ears caught the lively sounds of children, playing football on the grass across the road. They were shouting to each other, arguing about goals, enjoying the sunshine and generally making the most of the good weather, but the exuberant signs of life were barred from entering through Cassie's front door. The dark, window-less wood effectively prevented any light from reaching the stairs where Cassie huddled. It would be like this forever, she thought, her home would be a suffocating vacuum, where the sunshine was kept out. She wanted to go into the kitchen and yank open the back door and show her parents the world outside, but she could imagine their reaction. They'd just think it was a ploy to get out of doing her homework, Dad would yell, and mum would try to placate, and then everyone would get upset; it was hopeless.

There was nothing for it but to go and write her story. Slowly she trailed to the bottom of the stairs to locate her school bag. She soon retrieved it, from the place where it had landed, when she had unceremoniously flung it down the night before. She pulled out a PE bag and left it on the floor, then the lunch box and drink bottle, dropping them next to the dirty clothes. At last she located the yellow book that Mrs Harrison had so painstakingly created. The bright colour encouraged her, and she was quite excited as she climbed the stairs again. She took some time in finding an ink pen, which she thought would better look the part, and then she cleared all the things from the top of her desk, by lifting them, en masse, onto her bed. Finally, she sat down to write.

Taking up the piece of scrap paper, on which she had written her beginning, she didn't know whether to laugh or cry. The writing was so indecipherable, it looked as if somebody had been using the paper to kill ants.

Cassie put her first draft to one side and opened the yellow book, smoothing out the pages carefully. The pristine white terrified her, what if she made a mess of it, what would Mrs Harrison say? She gritted her teeth in determination and thought about the Brontë's tiny books. She struggled to contain her impatient hand, her whole arm tensed as she forced her wrist into tight, unaccustomed movements. The process was painfully slow. Already, after just a few lines, her shoulder ached terribly, but the writing, she could see, was now tidy and tiny. At first glance, it looked incredibly off putting. It was like the copy of a page of 'The Secret', one of the Brontës' early stories, that Mrs Harrison had given them. Most of the class had put theirs on one side, not even attempting to decipher the black squiggles, but Cassie had been determined to try. It was a struggle to understand the minuscule print, but then by holding the book up to her nose, so that her eyes almost touched the paper, she had been able to read the words fairly clearly. She was just making out the first few phrases, when the sound of laughter had broken her concentration and she had dropped the book. Mrs Harrison had been highly amused.

"Our very own Charlotte Brontë look-alike, class." She had remarked, laughing aloud when she had seen Cassie's perplexed expression. "Charlotte literally had her nose in a book, Cassandra, according to one of her school fellows. Just let me get the exact quote." Rummaging through the pile of paperwork on her desk she picked up a book and quickly found the page she was looking for.

"We have Charlotte's friend Mary Taylor to thank for this kind observation." She noted, then, glancing round the class, to ascertain that she held everyone's full attention, she began to read.

"*When a book was given her, she dropped her head over it till her nose nearly touched it, and when she was told to hold her head up, up went the book after it, still close to her nose, so that it was not possible to help laughing*'. You can see Cassandra, why I was so struck by the resemblance." Cassie had smiled awkwardly but had not picked up the paper again. She was not particularly interested in the prose anyway, the first few lines had been about men sat in offices, and politics had never been a big pull to her whereas Jane Eyre's plight was of paramount importance. She loved reading about the girls at Lowood school; they felt real, especially Helen Burns. When Helen and Jane were talking about concentrating in class and Helen declares,

'*Your thoughts never seemed to wander while Miss Miller explained the lesson and questioned you. Now, mine*

continually rove away: when I should be listening...often I lose the very sound of her voice; I fall into a sort of dream.'
Cassie knew she could say exactly the same to Laura and it would be equally true; the knowledge made her thoughtful as she struggled over her book, fighting to control the pen, and wondering if it had been as difficult for Charlotte to write about her sister Maria, as it was for Cassie to write down all she could remember, about her time with Lizzie.

Chapter 23

Three weeks later, in the final week of term, Cassie sat at her desk, occupying the final minutes of the morning by watching white clouds moving over the rooftops of the houses opposite. Her mind had wandered again, because Mrs Harrison was teaching. Mr Field had been in for the first part of the morning, and Cassie had thoroughly enjoyed his lesson. The children had pushed all the desks and chairs to one side, and acted out role plays in the rest of the space. Mr Field had said they would remember their history better, and anyway, moving around would stop them from falling asleep. The class had loved it. Then Mrs Harrison had come back and the classroom was promptly returned to normal. Now, Cassie was looking out of the window, trying to decide whether any of the clouds looked like sheep. With a sickening feeling, she realised that Mrs Harrison was talking to her.

"Are you listening to me Cassandra Edwards?" Cassie blinked and blushed red, she had been trying so hard these last few weeks, and now she had messed it all up *again*. The only consolation was that she would soon be out of Mrs Harrison's class forever.

"No, Mrs Harrison," Cassie replied wearily. "I'm sorry."

"Truthful to the last!" Mrs Harrison commented, but smiled resignedly. "Now come and stand at the front where I can see you." With a sigh, Cassie stood up. As usual, she did so without pushing her chair back first, but, luckily, Laura was now sitting next to her, and she caught it quickly. The two girls exchanged smiles, then Cassie walked between the desks to stand next to the teacher.

"Now, class. Once again I have Miss Edwards up here and once again it is because of her exasperating daydreams. But that is where the similarities end. Miss Edwards and her absorption in her dream world have at times driven me, as Charlotte Brontë would say, *clean daft*, and I am the first to admit that she has tried my patience on numerous occasions." At this Cassie shifted uncomfortably, sweat pricked at the back of her neck and her feet ached.

"However," Mrs Harrison went on, "Cassie Edwards has written the most astonishing, moving and powerful piece of homework, I have ever read. "Talli's Secret" is a fictional account of a meeting with Charlotte Brontë, part of which took place on our very own school trip! She even wrote it in an exact copy of the minuscule Brontë script!" Mrs Harrison announced proudly. "Though how you knew that Charlotte's nickname was Talli, I don't know," the teacher added, in an aside to Cassie, who just smiled awkwardly and looked away.

"So, children, I was so impressed with this book that I gave it to a friend of mine to read and guess what? His company is going to publish it, so you're all going to be famous, even you, Brian Bottomley!"

"What? Clumsy Cassie?" A clear voice called out, but it went unnoticed, drowned out by the sound of the rest of the class cheering. Mrs Harrison folded her arms and smiled benevolently. Cassie just stood there, stunned, looking at the excited faces in front of her. For her, the news was taking some time to sink in, but most people were chattering exuberantly as soon as the cheers began to die down. Laura rushed forward and flung her arms around Cassie, and even Jason half got up, then sat down. He glanced at his friends, but they were already talking about film roles and took no notice of him, so he got up again and went forward to congratulate Cassie.

"Well done, you! That showed her!"

"Who?" Cassie grinned and they both turned round to look at Savannah, whose face was a picture of suppressed mortification. Cassie couldn't resist a smile as she saw the contortions Savannah's features were achieving in order to hide her horror, her brow furrowed with the strain. Savannah looked away when she saw Jason and Cassie staring, and she turned to talk to Poppy, but Poppy was talking to the girl on the other side of her and didn't even notice when Savannah nudged her.

After Cassie had had her moment of congratulation, Mrs Harrison sent Laura and Jason back to their seats.

"The rest of you get your maths books out. I'm doing an impromptu test." As the class let out a simultaneous groan, Mrs Harrison grinned and led Cassie towards the classroom door.

"Come with me, dear, I have a surprise for you." She smiled, indicating that Cassie should go into the corridor. Puzzled, Cassie walked slowly through the door and was shocked to find her parents waiting there. Lorna nervously clutched the handles of the wheelchair; Mike gripped the sides, his knuckles white. As Cassie walked towards them they were smiling weakly, but their eyes were wet. Mike put out his arms and Cassie stepped forward into them. Instantly her dad started to cry again, but he tried to talk as he sobbed.

"You wrote about her, *you wrote about her.*" He kept repeating. Cassie looked up at her mum to see her reaction. Lorna's eyes shone with tears, yet there was a glitter about them that had been missing for a long time. Lorna gazed down at her daughter tearfully, but when she spoke her voice was calm, without any of the tension that had been a part of it for so long. The determined cheerfulness, forced and fraudulent, had been swept away.

"I've been crying all morning," she said simply, "ever since Mrs Harrison called round, as soon as you'd left the house. She sat with me while I read that book."

"I'm so sorry, Mum, I didn't want you to be upset." Cassie replied quickly.

"No, Cassie, don't say sorry. It's me who should be sorry. I wouldn't even let you speak about Lizzie, your own sister. *As if she had never existed.*" Fresh tears burst out as Mike took her hand. Lorna's knees buckled and her body slumped forwards, on to Mike. She dropped her head down against his shoulder and pulled Cassie towards her, so that the three of them huddled together, clutching at each other as if they were drowning. They were there some fifteen minutes, before Mrs Harrison discreetly popped her head out of the classroom door and pointed in the direction of the Head teacher's office.

"I asked for it to be empty, so you can go down there. Cassie you remember the way, don't you? If you set off now, you should get there before the hordes are let loose. I'll join you in a few minutes, when I've dismissed the class for break." Lorna nodded and carefully turned the wheelchair round. They plodded off down the corridor.

"I didn't want to upset you, Mum," Cassie began,

looking earnestly up at her mother, tears streaking down both their cheeks.

"I know you didn't, love, but I think all that crying was a good thing actually. I was upset before, anyway. I just thought that if I pretended I *wasn't* then it might go away. It's been really, really hard for all of us, this charade that we are a normal happy family." Lorna's voice began to rise as she became more emotional; Cassie became alarmed. "We're *not* a normal happy family, we should face that! Lizzie's dead and your dad's in a wheelchair. I've been going crazy just trying to keep sane, and..."

"Hey!!!" Mike interrupted, "Hang on, love. You'll frighten Cassie! Let it out sure, but not all at once!" Lorna responded to the concern in Mike's voice and steadied herself, "Okay," she replied slowly, breathing more deeply and measuring her speech carefully. "Okay. Cassie, I'm sorry. Look, I want to be honest. I can't promise no more tears, I'm sure there's going to be lots of anger and tears to come, but I can promise, *no more silence.* We are going to remember Lizzie every day, the good things, and the bad. She wasn't perfect, Cassie. From what I read in this book, you seem to think she was completely faultless. You describe her as clever, caring and wonderful. She was wonderful, Cassie, she was our daughter, and that made her wonderful to us, but you're our daughter too, that makes *you* wonderful to us, no matter what you do. I want you to remember that. Stop thinking that you are second best! Is that a deal?" Lorna asked, stopping the wheelchair and bending down to look in Cassie's eyes, half mocking but deadly serious.

"A deal?" Cassie asked, nervously.

"Yes! You get to know how great you are, and how

much me and dad love you, but I'm allowed to rant and rave now and again, instead of being perfectly calm and placid, in the midst of all this!"

"What do I get to do then?" Mike queried, turning round awkwardly to look at Lorna and Cassie.

"You get to tell us how much you hate that wheelchair, but you *talk* about it, instead of going all moody and quiet. I know it's not much of a consolation, but maybe if you admit how dreadful it is, it will be easier for us to help."

"Oh." Mike fell into a resentful silence, which made Lorna angry again; she jolted the wheelchair forwards and banged it against the Head teacher's door, which Cassie hurriedly opened. The office was empty, as promised. Once she had shut the door firmly behind her Lorna continued.

"You want a miracle cure?" she levelled at Mike who looked away, embarrassed. His face was contorted in pain, but he remained silent.

"Of course you do," she went on, more gently, "So do I. I'd love it if you were the still the same man I married, the man who literally swept me off my feet. I'd give anything to have you back like that, for your own self esteem more than anything. You can still be that man if you let yourself, it's what's inside that counts."

"Rubbish!" Mike replied angrily. "That's utter rubbish," He repeated, bitterly. "To the whole world I am a cripple and nothing is going to change that."

"The world only looks at *what* you are, I'm talking about *who* you are!" Lorna yelled back, equally angrily. "The man inside that I fell in love with, the man that I have shared the past eighteen years with. Everything that makes you "*you*" is still there, inside. I still love *you*, with all my heart, but you don't love yourself." She stopped, Mike had begun crying.

"Of course I don't! How could anybody love this?" He asked, gesturing at his debilitated form.

" Easily, Mike," Lorna said firmly, "Because *we* do." She placed one arm around Cassie's shoulders, and bent to put the other round Mike. The release of her anger had given her strength. Cassie watched her father as he cried. She had been scared of him all her life, but now, seeing his tears, she drew closer to him and slid her hand in his. Mike clutched it and drew it to his face, snivelling noisily. His grip was tight and her hand was wet with tears and snot, but Cassie did not remove it. She leaned against her father and put her other arm round his shoulder, tears rolling down her face again. When Mrs Harrison opened the office door, she found them huddled together, crying. She watched in silence for a few moments, until her own eyes filled, then fury at her own behaviour burned her conscience. She looked again at the family, who had not noticed her entrance, and regret strengthened her resolve; closing the door quietly she went off to make some telephone calls.

Chapter 24

When Mrs Harrison joined the family, some time later, Cassie was astonished by the change in her teacher's manner. Gone was the frosty severity, and the fierce restrictions, instead Mrs Harrison was all warmth and enthusiasm in her efforts to assist Cassie and her parents.

"I hope you're all getting over the shock a little," she murmured apologetically as she entered the room.

"Please forgive me for the hasty fashion in which this has been arranged, Mr and Mrs Edwards, but you'll appreciate the time scales, with school holidays almost upon us." She looked to Mike for agreement but he was silent, still numbed with shock, his eyes red-rimmed; he gazed at Mrs Harrison without seeing her. Lorna, however was able to nod weakly, and the teacher took this as confirmation that she could continue. She gestured at the comfortable chairs placed before Mr Miller's desk, and carefully checked that the door to the secretary was still firmly shut, before seating herself in the Head's chair. She then waited until Lorna had sat down in the chair next to Mike's wheelchair, and Cassie had shrunk into place slightly behind her parents. When Lorna raised her eyes timidly to look at the teacher, Mrs Harrison smiled reassuringly at her, and Cassie, too, received a warm smile, which she shyly returned.

"Well," Mrs Harrison began, speaking rather quickly, but with a benevolent and friendly manner, punctuating her sentences with encouraging nods. "As you can imagine, when I received Cassie's homework in two weeks ago, I was *astonished*. At first I thought she must have copied it from somewhere, after all, she had never produced anything like that before. In fact, she'd never shown any interest at all in my class before we studied the Brontës. I could ask her the simplest question, one to which I was sure she would know the answer, and there would be nothing, her head would be pointed towards the window, and her thoughts tangled in daydreams. It used to drive me mad, because I was sure that if she tried harder she would be able to produce something, and this book has proved me right!" Mrs Harrison announced triumphantly, sliding 'Talli's Secret' with its bright yellow cover across the Heads desk. Lorna stared at it as if hypnotised, but Mike averted his eyes swiftly. Mrs Harrison paused but neither parent spoke, so she began again.

"As I told Cassandra's class this morning, I have a friend who will be willing to publish this book. Under a pen name of course," she added hastily, as Mike's eyes flashed angrily. "I think it would be of great benefit to Cassandra, a boost to her confidence if you like, to enable her to cope better with her difficulties."

"Difficulties?" Mike put in swiftly, his shoulders tensed in defence.

"Oh, not the difficulties with regard to, erm, your loss. I meant her other difficulties, the problems she has experienced in class. I've been on the telephone this morning to the Educational Psychologist, Miss Nussey, and going from what I've told her, she thinks it *is* likely that Cassandra has a condition called dyspraxia, and possibly mild dyslexia as well. Obviously, we will have to get a proper diagnosis, but it certainly would explain much of her behaviour, the poor hand writing for one thing, the clumsiness, the problems she has with co-ordination, and of course the daydreams. Dyspraxic children are quite often characterised as daydreamers." Mike and Lorna sat dazed as they struggled with this suggestion. Cassie listened closely; she leaned forward, nearly causing the chair to fall as she moved, her knuckles turning white as they gripped the edge of her seat.

"I've never even heard of dyspraxia or dyslexia. Does it mean that Cassie has brain damage?" Lorna asked anxiously. Mike's brow furrowed as he considered the possibility.

"No. As far as I've been told, neither condition is associated with a damaged brain. The brain is normal, except that, for some reason, it works a little differently in the way it passes information to itself. If you liken it to a car journey, you could say that whereas most people take the shortest, quickest route to get from A to B, children with dyspraxia take the scenic route. Sometimes, this includes a detour, or a stop to look at something of interest on the way. These brains can be among the most inventive and creative, because they find new pathways, and make connections that no one has ever thought of before. They're not wrong, just different."

"Is it my fault?" Lorna asked tentatively. Mrs Harrison smiled gently,

"No dear." She replied, watching for Cassie's reaction as her face peered round her mother's shoulder. "I don't believe there is a known cause, but you can ask all these questions when Cassie has her assessment. Miss Nussey told me that there are many successful people who happen to have dyspraxia or dyslexia, or both. In fact she recently read an article that suggested that the eldest Brontë, Maria, may also have been dyspraxic. The article, used the description of Helen Burns that Charlotte Brontë has put in Jane Eyre, so that's a coincidence, isn't it Cassie?"

Mrs Harrison looked at Cassie and nodded encouragingly, Cassie nodded back, Mrs Harrison gave her pupil a warm smile and continued.

"One thing is for sure, there is absolutely nothing wrong with Cassie's intelligence. She could well be one of the brightest pupils in my class. She just hasn't had a chance to show it until now." Mrs Harrison gazed at Cassie, whose face expressed her growing excitement; her lips trembled and her eyes flashed brilliantly. Cassie spoke then, but it was still, as yet, in a hesitant, questioning manner.

"I'm not stupid, then?" She asked slowly, and then answered herself by repeating the words mechanically. "*I'm not stupid.*" Watching the growing realisation on her pupil's face, Mrs Harrison's heart filled with reproach. She stood up, walked round to stand before Cassie, and put her arms out to her. Cassie remained seated, shocked, and kept her head down, but it was raised slowly during Mrs Harrison's emotional apology.

"Cassandra, my dear. I blame myself for you even having to ask that question. No, a thousand times, no. *You are not stupid,* and I want to beg you to forgive me for treating you so. When I think of what I have been told this morning about Dyspraxia and Dyslexia, things I should have known already... well, I'm ashamed. I really am. Can you forgive me?" Cassie studied the figure stood before her; the drooping shoulders, the greying hair and the lined, once so fearsome, face. She looked at the outstretched hands, wavering more nervously the longer they waited. Remembered pain flashed through

195

her mind, but the incidents of humiliation and misery were swept away, by a rush of pity that flooded Cassie to the core. Immediately she got up from the chair and stepped forwards towards her teacher. Mrs Harrison's arms wrapped themselves round Cassie's shoulders and clung to her tightly. The teacher sobbed with relief, while simultaneously vowing promises of assistance, for as long as Cassandra and her family needed her. Mike and Lorna remained silent, each alone in their thoughts and barely aware of each other, they sat side by side, their fingertips entwined, staring, unseeingly, at a strangely familiar picture on the wall besides the window. Returning their gaze, from the safety of its wooden frame, the portrait of Charlotte Brontë smiled down enigmatically upon them.

Chapter 25

The school holidays were halfway through, and the events of the last few weeks of term now seemed like a distant dream to Cassie. Much of the time had been spent with Laura, and the pair were now firm friends, so much so, that when Laura's mother was arranging trips out, Cassie was always automatically included. Laura usually arrived full of excitement with her mother's plans, but one afternoon she called in a sombre mood. Cassie knew that Laura, though once so shy, was lively and vivacious when it was just the two of them alone, so she was surprised when the solemnity continued into her small bedroom, where they sat cocooned by CD's playing the girls' favourite music. She looked intently at Laura as she slumped on one end of the bed.

"You okay?" she asked simply. Laura gave a brief smile, but looked away, suddenly fascinated by a cuddly seal pup picture that had been in the same place all summer, without exciting any interest before.

"Yeah, I suppose."

"Why the long face then, bad news?"

"It's not meant to be, mum's organised us another day out."

"That's good, isn't it, or are you getting sick of me?" Cassie asked, sticking out her bottom lip in mock misery. Laura shook her head, but she didn't smile.

"She said she'd take us to Oakwell Hall tomorrow, some kind of activity day. I didn't know what to say."

"Oh," Cassie replied, looking down awkwardly and biting her bottom lip.

"You don't have to go if you don't want to," Laura added quickly. "I know it upset your dad last time. I'll say you're doing something else if you like."

"You'd be on your own then."

"Don't worry about it, I'll just have to make Mum do the crafts with me, that'll keep her quiet." The two girls laughed, Laura's mum was great at taking them out in the car, and buying drinks in cafes, but she steered clear of getting her fingers dirty, and avoided glue and glitter sessions whenever possible, waving her long manicured fingernails and muttering about slime.

"I'll go and ask mum, see what she says," Cassie decided and went off in search of her parents while Laura changed the music.

⋆　⋆　⋆

Mike and Lorna were in the dark front room when Cassie came down the stairs. She walked in slowly, surprised to find them there. She was even more astonished to see that Mike was busily packing up ornaments into a box on his knee, while Lorna was already stripping wallpaper, vigorously yanking each length and victoriously waving the pieces, before putting them in a black bin bag at her feet.

"What are you doing?" Cassie murmured, aware that it was a stupid thing to say, but wonderment making her witless. Her dad laughed.

"Now I know you don't learn anything at that school of yours. It's obvious we're decorating."

"But I thought..." Cassie began, hesitating, her eyes

filling. Her mum saw and came over. Lorna's eyes too welled up with tears, and they began to roll down her cheek, but she didn't hide them, she just smeared them across her face with the back of her hand.

"I know, darling, I know. But my two beautiful girls chose me some new wallpaper so why should I leave it in the cupboard? What would Lizzie think of that? We're not going to hide it away any more, we're going to hang it up, me and your dad, so that every time we see it in here, it will remind us of you both, flowers for our flowers." Mike was gulping in the corner and Cassie leaned against her mother, smelling the perfume Lorna had started wearing again, and feeling secure. She cried a little, and Lorna wiped her eyes casually, but didn't seem unduly perturbed. After a few minutes she lifted Cassie's head and smiled gently, her face was peaceful and her forehead no longer furrowed with frowns.

"We all miss her, Cass. We won't forget her, but she would want us to be happy. Don't you agree?" Cassie looked up and nodded, trying to smile; Lorna looked pleased.

"Now, what did you come down for? You've left poor Laura on her own upstairs." Immediately Cassie's whole demeanour altered, her face paled and she lost her relaxed expression. Mike and Lorna exchanged anxious glances.

"Laura's mum's organised us a trip, tomorrow, to Oakwell Hall." Mike's face grimaced and he turned away. Cassie looked terrified.

"I don't have to go, I'll tell her I can't." Lorna remained silent, but looked expectantly in her husband's direction. She knew it was something he had to deal with himself. She no longer attempted to pretend that he was unchanged since the accident, but nevertheless it was hard, she desperately wanted to protect him. She stared at his back, willing him to speak, and restraining herself from saying anything cheerful, or trying to gloss over it. It seemed to Lorna that her marriage, her life and her future, were all held in suspense while she and Cassie were waiting, eyes focused on the hunched back. She didn't realise she'd been holding her breath until Mike turned to speak to his daughter, and from deep in Lorna's lungs out came a loud exhalation of the old air. Mike glanced in her direction and pulled a face, scowling at the memories, only half-joking, before he turned back to Cassie.

"You want to go back to where they kicked your old dad out?" he smiled. "Well I can't say I wish I could come too!" He forced himself to laugh while Cassie watched anxiously, but, seeing her uncertain face, Mike modified his tone when he spoke again.

"It's nice you can go with Laura, love. At least I won't feel I'm holding you back." The words were spoken regretfully, but without rancour. The bitter bile of anger was gone, only a muted acceptance remained. Cassie hugged Mike and he squeezed her in silence, and then gently pushed her away with a smile.

"Now, back upstairs, see to your friend. Your mum and I have got work to do." Cassie nodded, and giving her Dad a final peck on the cheek, went off back upstairs to tell Laura the good news. Mike quickly dropped his head down to the box in front of him, and resumed his job of packing ornaments without looking at Lorna. She waited until Cassie had gone before going across to him, and putting her arms round his hunched shoulders.

"You did the right thing." She murmured.

"Its not easy." he muttered, his face still staring into the box, seeking refuge. Lorna stroked the back of his head, idly twisting the whorls of greying hair round her fingers. The sensuality of her touch calmed him, and his shoulders began to relax.

"I don't suppose it is, but you can tell me all about it tomorrow; we'll be alone all day."

"*Alone all day.*" Mike repeated, then he turned round to look at his wife, and he grinned cheekily. "Well, I could, or maybe we could find something better to do." Lorna raised her eye brows and smiled, then she kissed him, warmly and lingeringly. It was a few minutes before she went back to wrenching the wallpaper, still smiling.

Chapter 26

The weather forecast for the day of the visit was for violent thunderstorms, but when Laura and her mum called to pick up Cassie, the sun broke from behind the clouds and illuminated the jeep in a ray of sunshine, making the silver paintwork quite dazzling. Lorna stood at the front door to wave Cassie off.

"You look like Cinderella off to the ball in that glittering coach," she laughed,

"Mum! People will hear!" Cassie warned, but she was smiling. Lorna disappeared back into the house and found Mike peering out at the street, from behind the thick net curtains of the front room.

"Once those go you won't be able to hide any more," Lorna commented.

"Better make the most of it while I can then," Mike replied, trying to smile, but uncomfortably aware that it was hardly a joking matter. They both knew how difficult it was for him to meet new people; he couldn't shake off the belief that they always looked at the wheelchair first, and last, and quite often skipped the middle bit, the person in it, entirely. Initially, Lorna had tried to dissuade his viewpoint, but, after several months of pushing Mike around in the wheelchair, she had come to the depressing conclusion that he was right; sales assistants in shops who previously made a beeline for her tall, athletic husband as soon as he strode through the shop doorway, now gave them ample time to look around;

when they did finally approach they spoke only to Lorna, leaving her to struggle in alien territory while Mike maintained a dour silence.

★ ★ ★

The journey to Oakwell was uneventful, which came as a relief to Cassie. She and Laura chattered happily all the way, discussing their favourite groups, what was in the new issue of the magazine they both enjoyed reading and so on, until they joined the country lane leading to the Hall itself, and Cassie fell silent. She found herself nervously straining to look round each bend for Savannah on her pony, but, this time there were no such interruptions, and the jeep was soon parked neatly adjacent to the sunny courtyard. Laura's mum quickly spotted the sign for the tearooms.

"Look, girls, there's a cafe up there. Why don't I get us a seat? You can come and join me as soon as you've finished your activities. Don't feel you have to rush, I've got some magazines in my bag; I'll sit outside and do a spot of sunbathing. Take your time and have fun!" She commanded. Before they had time to reply, Laura's mum had departed, her smart city shoes stumbling on the stony path, the girls looked at each other and grinned.

"Well at least she won't be standing over our shoulders and making comments." Laura remarked, gazing at the retreating figure.

"Or even worse, standing over our shoulders and making the things for us." Cassie smiled, then as the barn doors opened at the bottom of the courtyard, and a sudden surge of people pushed towards them, the girls were swept along, amidst a wave of anxious adults shepherding their vociferous charges.

Inside the barn were tables writhing with hands, feathers, glue, newspapers, string and other craft accessories. The usually benign influence of the adult aid, specially drafted in for the children's activity day, pervaded and ruled over all. The parents knew this and acted accordingly, to obtain the choicest craft items for their offspring. Cassie and Laura found themselves almost unable to gain a place at a table, until a kindly faced helper spotted them, and made a gap. For twenty minutes they twisted pipe cleaners and moulded plasticine. Thoroughly absorbed in the activity, despite the cacophony of sound, Cassie enjoyed sculpturing a small figure. She proudly displayed it to Laura.

"That looks like nothing on earth!" Laura said cheekily.

"Good, 'cause it's meant to be an alien!" Cassie replied quickly and both girls laughed. They began to admire each other's creations, but impatient voices from behind stilled their enthusiasm.

"Could you move away from the table if you've finished." A booming, command rang out right behind Cassie and Laura.

"Yes." A querulous voice added, "My poor little baby has had to wait ages." Cassie and Laura shared a glance, then shrugged and turned dutifully, expecting to see a small toddler. They looked down with a ready smile, but there was only a mass of long, blonde hair coming from someone the same size as themselves: Savannah.

Cassie gasped in astonishment; Savannah squirmed in embarrassment. Beside her stood both her doting parents, expensively dressed in wholly unsuitable clothes, a blue jacket and matching trousers for her father, and a smart designer suit in beige and gold for her mother. They looked totally out of place, among the earnest t-shirts and jeans of the rest of the adults around them. Glue and glitter already trailed down the mother's sleeve, which had so far gone unnoticed, while Savannah's father's bulk almost squeezed Savannah, breathlessly, against her mother in the crush of people. Savannah's mother took this as an indication that Savannah wanted a cuddle, and planted a huge kiss on the top of her daughter's head, Savannah's cheeks flushed red but she was, amazingly, silent, and pretended not to recognise Laura and Cassie.

"This way, ladies," Savannah's father said loudly, gesturing to Cassie and Laura to come through, although he was virtually impassable, "then my own little lady can pass through and start her *masterpiece*." His voice was reverberating about the small barn, several parents turned to stare; Savannah's parents seemed to relish the attention. Cassie and Laura grinned at Savannah, she stared icily back at them. Just as Cassie thought Savannah might give in and say something the deep voice shook her again.

"Say, don't I know you little lady?" Savannah's father asked, "Ain't I seen you somewhere?" Cassie looked up in surprise.

"No," she said.

"Yes, I know you, you must be one of my Savannah's playmates. Aren't you one of the ones that's seen Savannah's pony?" Cassie couldn't lie, she shot a glance at Savannah, convinced Savannah would say something about Cassie's dad's car nearly hitting her pony last time they had come to Oakwell, but although Savannah bit her lip speculatively she looked rather more nervous than threatening.

"I *have* seen Savannah's pony," Cassie said carefully.

"I knew it!" Savannah's dad said triumphantly, addressing the whole barn; other parents smiled and nodded politely while he beamed, puffing his chest out proudly, "Didn't I say Mildred? I never forget a face." Savannah's mum nodded.

'*Mildred*' Cassie mouthed to Laura. Savannah was furious but said nothing.

"Yes, Harold, you're right again."

'*Harold*' Laura mouthed back; Cassie smiled, but then jumped, when Savannah's father addressed her again in his strident voice.

"You might be one of Savannah's friends, but I think I've seen you somewhere else, something to do with school, now let me think."

He paused, and the barn paused too, Savannah appeared positively agitated.

"Ah-ha!" He said at last. "You're the girl who wrote the book for her school homework!"

"Savannah told you about my book?" Cassie was astonished; she looked at Savannah, but Savannah dropped her gaze and stood chewing her bottom lip. The echo was going round the barn.

"Wrote a book for her homework." Parents muttered to each other, their gaze dropping to their offspring hopefully; the parents of the smallest, finding it easier to anticipate that their child would grow up and emulate the young author.

"Savannah didn't *actually* tell me." Savannah's father admitted. "I saw it in the local paper. A little article, very small, and a rather grainy school photograph to accompany it. I have to say that when *my Savannah* is in we like to make sure it's a good picture. I get a professional to do it for me, before we send them in. Anyway, it was better than some I've seen. After all I managed to recognise you. Didn't you see it?"

"No. We don't get that paper."

"I'm sure Savannah could bring it to school for you," Savannah's father said generously, "after all that business with the bullying."

"*Savannah told you about the bullying?*"

"Well, we had to prise it out of her but she admitted it in the end." Cassie was astounded; she looked at Savannah almost with respect, but Savannah wouldn't meet her eye.

"I can't believe she told you."

"Well it was after I showed her that article, and I asked her about you. There was a line or two about bullying and she said yes she knew you, and when I asked her why she hadn't told me about the bullying, she said at first she didn't want to talk about it, but then she admitted that yes, she'd been bullied."

"*She'd been bullied?*" Cassie repeated dumbly,

"Yes, by the same girl that bullied you, the one you wrote about in your book."

"The one I wrote about in my book?"

"Yes, you know, it said in the paper you wrote about the kid that had bullied you in this book. Someone called Brontë had done the same I think, written about bullying at school, that's what gave you the idea the paper said." Savannah's father stared at Cassie oddly, "Don't you remember what you wrote?"

"Yes, of course," Cassie replied.

"So you must know the kid I'm talking about, this girl that you put in the book."

"Oh, yes. Have you read the book?"

"Nooo!" the loud voice boomed, and Savannah's father laughed as if Cassie had made a brilliant joke. "I don't have time to *read*, busy men like me leave reading for you kids in school, but I am going to buy it for Savannah, and she can tell me what's in it."

Cassie looked at Savannah, who had the grace to look embarrassed.

"I know the paper said you have had to change names for publication, dear," Savannah's mother began hesitantly. "But I've been terribly worried about this bully and I would like to know who it is, so that I can speak to their parents." Cassie and Laura looked incredulously at each other. Savannah's father quickly agreed,

"Yes, I wanted to ask you myself," he blustered. "I've often said, haven't I Mildred, I wish I had that girl in front of me right now. The things I'd say to her! Bullying is for cowards and wimps!" He shouted, becoming expansive, he had quite an audience.

"I'd tell her that bullies are *miserable* and *nasty* inside, where it counts. They have to be, if their only pleasure is picking on nice kids like you." He smiled jovially at Cassie, ruffling Savannah's blonde hair. Other adults were gazing on approvingly, Savannah's father smiled benevolently at them all.

"Come on, honey," he said to Cassie, "I can stop this for you. I'll make sure that bully doesn't ever pick on you again, or on my little Savannah here."

"I don't think there is any danger of that," Cassie said, winking at Laura.

"Don't be scared of telling us, dear," Savannah's

mother urged.

"Oh, I'm not scared at all," Cassie retorted boldly. Savannah's head shot up, and her expression was that of desperation. She was pleading with Cassie not to speak. Cassie paused, and opened her mouth, Savannah looked terrified; Cassie felt sorry for her.

"But I've signed a secrecy thing with my publisher," she said, airily. "Specifically relating to privacy, etc. Sorry I can't help." Savannah was relieved; Cassie smiled at her, but Savannah turned away.

"But aren't you worried that the bullying might start up again, once all this dies down?" Savannah's father asked. Cassie stared at the back of Savannah's head, still turned to gaze at the other end of the barn.

"I don't think that will happen at all," Cassie answered calmly. "Do you Savannah?" The question was loud and direct, and Savannah had to turn round, but she couldn't bring herself to look Cassie in the face, her gaze hovered over the small figure Cassie still clutched in her hand. Savannah's parents looked at their daughter anxiously, Savannah's reply, when it came, could barely be heard.

"No, it's all finished now, there won't be any more bullying." Laura and Cassie smiled at each other.

"You see how all this has affected her," Savannah's mother said, smoothing her fingers over her daughter's blonde hair, all the way from her head to her waist. "She used to be so outgoing and now she's so quiet. *My poor, poor baby.*" Savannah shook off her mother's hand irritably and assumed a sullen pout.

"We ought to let Cassie go now, Mum."

"Yes of course, darling." Savannah's mother looked at her daughter affectionately. "You're always so thoughtful, always thinking of others. Is she like that at school?"

"Always thinking of others?" Cassie and Laura smiled in unison. "Oh, absolutely, Mrs Smythely. In fact, you could almost say, it's a fault." Savannah pulled a face, she knew when she was beaten.

"It's been a pleasure to see you, little miss." Savannah's father said grandly, offering his hand. Cassie took it and shook it warmly.

"The pleasure's all mine, I'm sure. 'Bye Savannah, see you back at school." She grinned, and, linking arms with Laura, set off through the crowd of people, who parted politely to let the girls pass through. When they were gone, Savannah lifted one arm pathetically up to her father's shoulder, and bent him towards her, while she looked up with huge eyes, still slightly nervous.

"Do you know, Dad, I'm not sure I'm as strong as Cassie. I don't think I want to go back to that school after the holidays. Do you think I could change schools?" Both parents looked at their daughter with smothering concern, Savannah's mother began in her querulous voice.

"I knew all this bullying had affected her badly, she used to have such fun and games at that school, and now look at her."

"Don't worry, pumpkin." The booming voice of Savannah's father rattled around the barn again, so that Laura and Cassie heard it just as they were about to go outside. "You can change schools if you want to, Daddy will sort it out!"

"Good old daddy!" Cassie laughed.

"No more Savannah!" Laura grinned. "This calls for a celebration!" Laura's mum was soon located, sitting with a coffee and a couple of magazines in the garden of the café. She happily gave them some money for ice cream, and pointed in the direction of the ice cream van.

"Are you going to sit with me, or shall I look after your models while you go for a wander? I know you young people might find it boring sitting here." She looked hopefully at the girls; she had just refilled her coffee and got another magazine out of her bag.

"We'll have a walk, mum, if you're sure you don't mind."

"I know a cool place where we can eat our ice creams," Cassie said.

"*Cool* place," Laura's mum laughed. "Good joke, Cass. Alright, you run along and I'll make sure the models dry properly."

"That's mum's idea of babysitting," Laura laughed, as they paid for the ice creams. "Bits of plasticine that don't move or speak. Should we tell her that plasticine doesn't need to dry?"

"No, let's leave her in peace. Come on, I'll show you the best bench to eat these on." Cassie murmured. They walked away from the ice cream van, across the avenue, and up the stony path to the Hall.

"Are we going in?" Laura asked nervously, looking at the dark exterior with little enthusiasm.

"Do you want to?" Cassie asked, smiling to herself.

"No thanks, it looks haunted if you ask me, I bet some old ghost walks up here when the full moon is up..."

"Funny you should say that." Cassie laughed, leading Laura up a path at the side of the house.

"Oh, look, Cass, they must be doing activities inside the Hall as well." Laura pointed in at a small window, through which Cassie could see three figures in brilliant pinafores; they were quietly occupied at one end of the Dining Table. She recognised the figure of Talli's friend,

211

Mrs Cockill.

"Can you see those people clearly, Laura?" Cassie asked her friend, Laura nodded eagerly.

"Oh, yes. I mean, I can't see exactly what it is they're doing, do you think we'd be able to have a go?"

"I think that activity might be just for the school pupils," Cassie said with a smile.

"Oh, is it a school then?" Laura asked innocently.

"It has been for a very long time," Cassie replied. "Come on, I think there's someone to meet you up here." The two girls went through a gate and found themselves in the beautiful gardens at the back of the Hall; Cassie led Laura up the gravel paths to the very end of the walled garden. The solitary bench by the apple trees was empty and Laura sat down uncertainly.

"Are we allowed up here?" she asked, surveying the quiet gravelled walks and formal rose beds.

"Oh yes. Talli brought me here last time. It's so peaceful. She said she often visits here."

"Talli?" Laura asked nervously.

"Charlotte Brontë. You saw her too, remember?" Laura was now a ghostly white, her hands trembled and she shivered involuntarily.

"But I thought that was just someone dressed up," she said slowly. Cassie looked at her, perplexed.

"I thought you knew, after you read my book. I thought you must have realised."

"I thought it was just a story." Suddenly the two girls eyes met, and the mirrored shock made them both laugh suddenly.

"That's nice to hear." A voice said behind them, and they both turned to recognise the figure at the same time.

"Talli!" A girl had appeared from a gate, in the wall at the back of the garden; the gate was almost hidden by the apple varieties trained along the stone. She wore clothes which camouflaged her again, but more cheerfully this time, soft green and peach for her dress, with an apricot coloured bonnet. As she stood before them, she seemed to melt into the rose bushes in the sunshine, only gaining more solidity when the increasing clouds passed before the sun.

"It's good to see you again Cassandra," Talli addressed her formally, with a deep bow, but then sweeping formalities aside as she swept her skirts she smiled, and added, "Or should I say Cassie, since you call me Talli in your book?"

"You know about my book?" Cassie asked incredulously.

"Of course," Talli nodded, her eyes twinkling, "and I'm guessing this is your very good friend, whom you renamed Ellen, just like my friend. May I join you?"

"Yes!" both girls said, at exactly the same time, which made them both laugh again.

"This is Laura," Cassie said eagerly.

"Hello Laura," Talli said, smiling at Laura's consternation. Laura was open-mouthed with surprise but she didn't feel scared. She was aware that *technically* she was talking to a ghost, but this friendly apparition was no relation at all to the ghouls of gothic horror movies. It was like meeting an ordinary person, *almost*, Laura thought, but she couldn't bring herself to speak, her mouth was too dry. Talli seemed to find it most amusing. "Quiet type, is she?" She asked, her bright eyes twinkling mischievously. "Silent as the grave, perhaps?"

"Honestly, Talli!" Cassie scolded playfully, "Never

mind poor Laura for now. How do you know about my book?"

"You could say I'm your guardian angel. I knew you were coming here today, so here I am. You're looking much happier, Cassie." Cassie smiled, the golden hue pervading her features, as it had once done for Talli in the very same garden.

"I am happier," Cassie acknowledged simply, "Writing that book changed my life, Talli."

"I know exactly what you mean, writing Jane Eyre changed mine." Talli agreed. "Not just for the money, or the little bit of fame I tried so carefully to avoid, but the way I could work from then on. Writing was a gift to take my mind away from other things." Cassie nodded.

"Yes, I still think of Lizzie, I miss her terribly."

"Of course you will. You can't avoid these times, if you tried to run away from them who knows what weird feelings would follow?" Talli smiled pensively. "But at least now when things get bad you have The Secret."

"The Secret?" Laura asked, puzzled.

"Laura finally managed to speak!" Cassie laughed, "Alright then Laura, how's this for a secret, Scribblemania!"

"Scribblemania?" Laura asked, even more confused. "What on earth is that?" Cassie and Talli smiled at each other then turned to Laura, and talking together at the same time, half-shouted.

"*When you are going to write because you just cannot help it!*" Laura looked at them perplexed and they both started laughing.

"But what good would that do?" Laura asked. Talli and Cassie stopped laughing, and sighed; Talli looked suddenly solemn.

"I lost my siblings, Laura, *one by one*, and no words can describe how awful it is, but the very act of writing helped me out of that dark and desolate reality into a happier region. It was a relief to write it down, it would have caused great pain to talk it over. When I wrote Jane Eyre, and thought up the character of Helen Burns, I remembered Maria, and in putting parts of her life in the book I felt she wouldn't be forgotten. How should I have survived otherwise?" She paused, thoughtful. "Seeing Cassie that day in the Parsonage, brought all that back to me, and I resolved to help the only way I knew how." She spoke solemnly, but then as the clouds parted from the sun, and a shaft of light illuminated the bench where the girls were seated, her tone changed and she became vibrant again. "And how well it worked! It has driven me clean daft!" she added, laughing, and a rumble of thunder above seemed to echo her amusement. She looked up to the sky, "Well it appears I have to be going; they're waiting for me."

"Who?" Cassie asked, puzzled.

"Why my family of course, my sisters, my brother, Papa, Mama. We're all together. That's my real Secret for you, Cassie, and it has to stay a secret. When I was left alone, I missed them all terribly, but I couldn't bring them back. At times it grew so desperate I would try with all my might to look beyond the grave, and I didn't know where to turn. I felt that if there were no hope beyond this world, no eternity, no life to come, it would be heartbreaking. That's why I want you to know that you will meet Lizzie again, she's waiting for you, and she wanted me to tell you she loves your book, and what it's done for your mum and dad. She's really proud of you."
Talli stopped because Cassie was now crying desper-

ately, her body shaking and sobbing. Laura held her and looked to Talli helplessly. Talli lifted her hand slightly towards Cassie. "You have written something of great value and you can do much more. Remember Scribblemania – don't stop writing, write about everything and anything, let it soothe your mind, excite your mind..."

The thunder boomed and Talli's words were deafened, a warning wind was swirling rose petals across Talli's face and shielding it. There was no rain just yet but the rumbling from above made her look up and hurry her speech; addressing herself to Laura's appeal she spoke quickly but kindly.

"Friendship is a plant which cannot be forced, Laura, but grows over time. A seed has been sown and is flourishing, I am glad to see. You and Cassie will derive great solace from your mutual regard; she doesn't need me anymore."

"Will I see you again?" Cassie asked, raising her head as Talli started to walk towards the apple trees, fading as she passed them.

"No, Cass, this is goodbye." Cassie jumped to her feet, the first raindrops were starting to fall, several landed, disregarded on Cassie's cheeks and mingled with the tears, washing them away.

"Wait!"

"I must go," Talli said, and indeed, she was slipping into the orchard and disappearing as she spoke, her voice could barely be heard between the rolls of thunder.

"But no matter what, Cassie, don't stop. *Remember Scribblemania, Talli's Secret.*" Then, Talli's figure faded completely into the greens, and large, oddly luminous, drops of rain began to drop heavily onto the two girls.

The wind was blowing the rose petals wildly around them, some stuck to their hair and faces, making them laugh.

"Come on, Cassie, time to move on." Laura smiled. Cassie gave one last look into the trees but there was nothing to be seen. She grabbed Laura's hand and the two of them ran through the garden, shrieking and laughing, as they dodged rain drops and rose petals. As they headed for the gateway, there was one last whistling breeze which gusted from behind them, and propelled them towards the café and Laura's mother. The warm wind was so strong it felt like hands pushing at their backs, and afterwards Cassie and Laura agreed they'd both heard the sound of children laughing as the echo of Talli's last words seemed to whisper through the garden,

"Remember Scribblemania, Talli's Secret."

Bibliography

If, having read *Talli's Secret*, you now have an interest in the Brontës' and their work then firstly, I am delighted, and secondly, here are some useful books:

Jane Eyre by Charlotte Brontë... you will know the start of this already!

Shirley by Charlotte Brontë... has a good description of Oakwell Hall in it.

The Brontës by Juliet Barker, which is an amazing biography of the Brontë family, includes: information about the School described in *Jane Eyre* and the creation of the Brontë children's books as Mrs Harrison tells Cassie's class in *Talli's Secret*. Lifelong friend Mary Taylor's first impressions of Charlotte Brontë when they met. Charlotte was fourteen years old, shy, nervous, and spoke with a strong Irish accent.

The Brontës: A life in Letters also by Juliet Barker, Charlotte writes of Scribblemania in her Roe Head Journal, October 1836. The letter from Robert Southey, dated March 1837, is also in there.

Juvenalia 1829–1835 by Charlotte Brontë edited by Juliet Barker
The introduction describes how the size of the

"minuscule print" in the small hand-made books contributes to the secrecy of the children's activities. "The imaginary world that the young Brontës had invented was therefore *a secret.*" (my italics). Included in this volume are several of the magazines which the Brontë children wrote, including a story by Charlotte in character as the *Chief Genius,* "Talli."

Life of Charlotte Brontë by Elizabeth Gaskell. This biography was written by a literary friend of Charlotte, Mrs Gaskell, who had visited the Parsonage. Some say this is a rather prejudiced account; certainly Mrs Gaskell knew how to write a good story.

Information about Dyspraxia and Dyslexia

Should be available from libraries, the internet, your GP or health visitor, school psychologist, etc or you can contact the following:

Dyspraxia Foundation
8 West Alley
Hitchin
Herts
SG5 1EG
Tel: 01462 454986 Helpline 10am–1pm, Mon–Fri
           01462 455016 Administration
Fax: 01462 455052
Website: www.dyspraxiafoundaton.org.uk

The Dyspraxia Foundation is a national, registered charity no 1058352

Dyslexia Institute
133 Gresham Road
Staines
TW18 2AJ

Tel   01784 463851
Website: www.dyslexia-inst.org.uk

The Dyslexia Institute is a registered charity no 268502